THE DAY I WASHED MY FACE IN THE TOILET

Brenda Kearns

Library and Archives Canada Cataloguing in Publication

Kearns, Brenda, 1963-, author
    The day I washed my face in the toilet / Brenda Kearns.

Issued in print and electronic formats.
ISBN 978-1-927711-04-0 (pbk.).--ISBN 978-0-9918114-2-7 (pdf)

        I. Title.

PS8571.E355D39 2014   jC813'.54   C2014-907650-9
                                                C2012-908538-3

—

Also by Brenda Kearns:

Home
Sleepover Zoo
There's Nothing Wrong With Claudia
Parrots and Popcorn

Ediciones en español:
El día que me lavé la cara en el inodoro
Fiesta de pijamas en el zoológico
No hay nada malo con Claudia
Pericos y palomitas de maíz

Éditions françaises:
Le Jour où je me suis lavé la figure dans la cuvette
Pyjamazoo
Claudine ne fait jamais rien de mal
Pop-corn et perroquets

For my mom and dad. Thanks for not killing me when I was a teen, even though I'm sure you wanted to.

TABLE OF CONTENTS

Chapter 1 7

Chapter 2 16

Chapter 3 28

Chapter 4 37

Chapter 5 45

Chapter 6 53

Chapter 7 63

Chapter 8 72

Chapter 9 83

Chapter 10 92

Chapter 11 99

Chapter 12 109

Chapter 13 118

Epilogue 129

Chapter 1

We Call Him Dementia Boy

Edward was naked, of course, except for the polka dot bandana he always wore like a mask on these special occasions. And he was using the upstairs bathroom window, this time — the puny one over the toilet — so I should have been spared the worst of the show. No such luck. By climbing on the toilet and turning his back to the window, he could press his butt against the glass, mooning me (and anyone else who happened to be looking). Then he'd crouch, spin around and wave — Dementia Boy in a polka dot mask — before starting his I'm-a-dork routine all over again.

Butt...polka dots...butt...polka dots...

If anyone discovered a drug that could cure what was wrong with my brother, they'd make millions.

"Oh, they'll be fine on the plane alone," Mom said. "Monica's 14, now, so she can keep an eye on Edward...can't you, Monica?" Mom was looking at me and smiling, but not with her real smile. It was her tight, fake smile. It was her *If old Mrs. Frieson sees what Edward's doing in that window, she's going to have another stroke* smile.

"Besides, it's only eight hours to England — he'll probably sleep through most of it," she added, nodding like mad, trying to get me to agree.

Butt...polka dots...butt...polka dots...

"Sure, Mom, he'll have no trouble sitting still for eight hours, as long as we kill him, first," I said.

Okay, that's what I *wanted* to say. Instead, I just smiled — my own version of the tight, fake smile — as I slowly shuffled to the left, trying to get old Mrs. Frieson between me and the window so she'd have her back to Dementia Boy. Mom shuffled along the sidewalk beside me, following my lead. It looked like a scene from one of those wild animal shows where a predator slowly circles its prey...except *these* predators were two crazed, smiling idiots, and the prey was a balding 82-year-old woman hunched over a walker.

Butt...polka dots...butt...polka dots...

"Well, I just don't think it's smart to let children fly all that way on their own," said Mrs. Frieson. She glared at my shuffling feet, then moved her walker so she could face us again.

"Mom's flying over in a couple of days, after her last surgery," I said. "And we're staying with my grandma. We'll be fine." My mom's a pediatric gastroenterology nurse. That means she takes care of kids after doctors have been poking around in their bellies trying to make their intestines work properly. You don't want the details, believe me.

Butt...polka dots...butt...polka dots...

"But where does your grandmother live? Is she near the

airport? How will you even find her? This is ridiculous!" Mrs. Frieson thumped her walker on the sidewalk for emphasis — I hadn't seen her this wound-up since she found Edward's dead spider collection in the mailbox.

If I'd had the nerve, I'd have told her it was none of her business. After all, she's only our landlady. But I didn't have the nerve. And she's our landlady.

"She's in a little town called Old Warden, near Bedford," Mom said. "And she'll pick them up at the airport. It's really no problem."

Mom's fake smile slid off her face as the bathroom window flew open.

"Actually, Old Warden isn't a town, it's a village!" Edward yelled through his polka dot mask, his scrawny chest hanging out the window. Even if puberty was incredibly kind to him, Edward was never going to be Tarzan material. "In England, a group of houses is called a hamlet. If there's a church, it's called a village. If there's a market, it's called a town. If there's a cathedral, it's called a city..."

Mrs. Frieson stared up at Edward with that glazed-over look that people get whenever he starts spouting facts. If there's anything worse than a demented kid, it's a demented kid who's also a walking dictionary.

Suddenly, her eyes flew open. "Is that boy *naked?*" she asked.

"Um, well, yes...he's...he's a little precocious," Mom said. As if on cue, Mom and I both made a break for it, scuttling toward the front door. "I have to get these kids packed!" Mom called over her shoulder. "Have a great weekend!"

"Precocious! What's *that* supposed to mean?" Mrs. Frieson called out.

"It means he's a pain in the neck," I muttered, as I latched the door shut behind me.

Mom ran up to the bathroom to make Edward put on his clothes. Seriously, how many 10-year-olds do you know who need to be told to wear clothes? If he wasn't such a great chess player, I would have drowned him in the tub years ago.

I'd had enough drama, so I went to my room to get packed. Big mistake.

The smell of hair spray took my breath away. Probably a good thing, too, because what I *wanted* to say wouldn't have scored any bonus points with "Please Get Along, Today" Mom. You've heard people talk about walking into a room where it looked like a bomb had gone off? Well, a bomb *had* gone off — a *bra* bomb. There must have been a dozen of them scattered all over the floor...plus a bright pink one dangling over my desk chair. *My* desk chair. And standing in the middle of the whole mess was Shelley, wearing the only bra she hadn't pitched across the room like a Frisbee.

"None of these stupid things fit anymore!" she yelled, waving her arms at her abandoned bra collection. "What am I supposed to do now?"

"Don't look at me," I muttered. I hooked one with my foot and kicked it onto her bed (I thought that added a nice dramatic touch, actually).

Okay, I suppose I could have been nicer. Having The Incredible Expanding Chest couldn't be easy. Shelley had officially reached the farthest edge of the sexy scale this year. Soon she'd be skidding right into "buxom cow" mode. But, really, she was asking the wrong person for sympathy. True, I was finally buying regular-sized bras. But I could probably still fit comfortably into my old training bra — not that I was going to depress myself by trying — and I probably wouldn't have had any trouble running *braless*, either.

It was as if the gene fairy had been sick and tired of

divvying things up fairly by the time she got to our family, so she just split the motherload right down the middle without giving it a second thought. Big boobs for Shelley...flat chest for me...long, slim legs for Shelley...short, dumpy legs for me...shiny blonde hair for Shelley...frizzy brown hair for me...perfect complexion for Shelley...straight A's for me...

Okay, so it wasn't entirely bad. Me and my dumpy legs had won the 8th grade science award this year — while there was a pretty good chance Shelley and her colossal boobs were going to end up working at some fast food joint after high school. But once (just once) I'd like to have to worry about whether a guy was only interested in me because of my looks. Seriously. Just once.

I made a sharp right and headed for my half of the room, holding my breath to avoid the hair spray fumes until I could get the window cranked open. Then I grabbed the bra she'd tossed onto my chair — *my* chair! — and sent it flying back onto her bed. The big ones fly surprisingly well.

Not that Shelley noticed. Now she was on a rampage, rummaging through her stuffed, overflowing dresser and muttering under her breath. But *loudly* under her breath, of course...one of Shelley's mottos: if you're going to rant, it's important to speak clearly so your unwilling audience can hear you.

"These are all old lady undies," Shelley complained, as she pulled out a baggy pair and shook them, hard, to knock off the socks that were stuck to them. Drama Queens love static cling — it really adds to their performance.

"Cripes, Shelley, we're only there for nine days — who's going to be looking at your underwear?" I asked. "Besides, you'd have tons to wear if you did your laundry once in a while."

"Aaaarrrggghhhh...there's lots *here*, it's just that none of it's *sexy*," she said, flinging a handful of mismatched socks over her shoulder. "We're going to London. I want to look sexy!"

"We're going to Old Warden," I muttered. "It's almost two hours away from London — read a map once in a while."

Shelley started throwing clothes into her suitcase — and when I say throwing, I mean *throwing*. Shelley didn't believe in folding anything. I opened the top drawer of my dresser. Bras on the left, underwear stacked neatly in the middle, socks in layers on the right. Why couldn't Shelley see how much easier life was when you could actually *find* things — like socks that matched and bras that fit? Why couldn't she see how much *nicer* things looked when they were organized?

Mom scurried past the door with Edward's suitcase. "Please do *not* let Auntie Gay bully you into packing up Grandma's things before I get there," she said. "Grandma's really upset about the idea of moving into an old folk's home, so I want to smooth things over before we ask her to make any changes."

Close behind her — crouched low and scuttling down the hall warrior-style — was Edward. He was wearing a black t-shirt, black shorts, black socks and a black cape. He had his old bow and a bunch of arrows tucked under his arm (not real arrows, of course — Mom's not nuts — *his* arrows had suction cups on the tips). As Edward followed Mom silently past the door, he never even glanced in to see what Shelley and I were doing. He never took his eyes off of Mom's back. Stealth Boy had targeted his prey.

I tucked two bras, five pairs of undies and five pairs of socks into the corner of my suitcase. I'd pack light and use Grandma's washer.

"Crap!" Shelley had yanked her sweater drawer out so far that it had dropped right onto her foot. Apparently, even divas need to show some restraint.

"And *please* don't let Auntie Gay make you do a ton of work to get things ready for her wedding," added Mom, as she raced past the door with an armload of Edward's clothes. "Honestly, I think she's lost her mind — having such a huge wedding when she's 64...it's silly!" Stealth Boy followed close behind, bow and arrow poised.

I slid the second drawer open. T-shirts. All folded neatly and color-coded, lightest ones on the left, darkest ones on the right. I pulled out one of each color so I could be sure to blend in.

"She's already picked out matching bridesmaid dresses for us — can you imagine?" Mom called from Edward's room. "She hasn't even *seen* you in four years. What makes her think she knows...Ouch! Dammit, Edward! Put those arrows away right now!" Stealthboy had struck.

Third drawer. Sweaters. Favorites folded neatly on the left. Baggy, premenstrual, "don't look at me I feel ugly today" sweaters on the right. I pulled out two of my favorites — no risk of PMS this week, and from what Mom had seen on the weather channel, it was going to be pretty warm over there, too.

"I *hate* packing!" Shelley muttered. No kidding. Now she was on her hands and knees, pulling dirty jeans and shirts out from the back of the closet. "I'll be doing laundry all night — you just watch!" I had no intention of watching, actually.

Bottom drawer. Pants and shorts. This one was easy. Shorts meant shaving — a *lot* of shaving. Ankles to undies shaving. Wearing pants meant just mowing down the worst of the fuzz tonight, then one more touchup the day of Auntie Gay's wedding. I picked out my three best pairs of jeans. Done — except for the bathroom stuff, of course.

Thunk!

I have to admit, Edward is fast. I yanked the plastic arrow

off my forehead and threw it back at him as I headed down the hall. True, there was a chance he'd shoot me again. But there was also a chance he'd go after Shelley, instead — and I'd always wondered what he'd look like with his head stuck in the toilet.

Our bathroom...picture a tiny room crammed with everything they sell in Walmart's beauty department, then add enough bathtub toys to make Mickey Mouse vomit, and you've pretty much got it pictured.

The tub was *half full* of old, faded, water toys — one of the many things that Edward was obsessed with and simply could *not* throw out. And then there were the baskets — six of them crammed onto the tiny countertop, overflowing with Shelley's nail polish, makeup and skin care stuff. Plus a blow dryer, a straightener (for when she hates her hair because it's too wavy), a curling iron (for when she hates her hair because it's too straight), brushes, combs, gels, clips...

Seriously, if you wanted to know what color the counter was, you'd need a shovel.

Mom and I have one drawer each. And that's enough, too. All I desperately need are my tweezers. If not for my tweezers, I'd have one big furry eyebrow — like a dead ferret draped across my forehead.

I quickly packed — brush, hair bands, soap...you know the drill — then headed downstairs. My toothbrush could wait until after breakfast tomorrow. Until then, I'd keep it tucked away in its usual safe spot at the back of my drawer. And actually, that's not as weird as it sounds. True, most people leave their toothbrushes on the counter, but think about it: there's a *toilet* in the bathroom, and every time someone flushes it, bacteria fly up into the air. Do you want your toothbrush lying there with toilet water raining down on it? That's disgusting. No, mine stays hidden at the back of my drawer. Mine stays clean, thanks.

Bang! Bang! Bang! Bang!...

I raced down the last few stairs just in time to see Mom throw open the front door. It was old Mrs. Frieson. Her hair — what was left of it, anyway — had been blown straight up by the wind. Her face was bright red. Her baggy old sweater was falling off her shoulders and she was holding onto her walker with one hand and waving a crooked finger at Mom with the other. She didn't look like she was going to have a stroke, anymore — she looked like she'd just *had* one.

"That boy of yours is on the roof," she sputtered. "And he's *naked again*!"

Chapter 2

The Longest Day Of My Life

Getting Edward down had been surprisingly easy. Shelley and I had both agreed — for a change — that Mom should call the fire department and have them hose him right off the roof. And considering all the trouble he'd caused on his class trip to the fire station, they probably would have done it, too. (Lesson #1 for all the dorky brothers out there: when your class goes on a field trip, do *not* spend the whole day interrupting the tour guide to spout historical facts — and never, *ever* push the button on the fire hall's smoke detector.)

But in the end, Mom ignored us and did what she usually does when Edward crosses the line. She put on her angry face — the one that makes a freakishly deep crease between her eyebrows — and hissed at him. That's right — she *hissed* at him to get off the roof. Now, Edward's a weird little nut, but he's not stupid. Even *he* knows that when Mom's got that forehead furrow and she's hissing, you'd bloody well better figure out what you've done wrong — and *un*do it — fast.

So there I was, just one day later, trying to survive the worst eight-hour flight I was ever going to endure in my entire life. True, it was the *only* flight I'd endured up to that point. But I was already pretty sure that if I ever went anywhere on a plane again...*ever*...even if the plane crashed in a fiery heap in the Arctic and we were eaten alive by polar bears, flying to England would *still* rank as the worst experience of my life.

You think I'm being melodramatic? Well, you're wrong. I really don't want to dwell on this, so here's a quick rundown — you can fill in the gory details, yourself:

2:45 a.m.

Mom woke us up. Not with her usual sugary-sweet *"Rise and shine. It's time for school,"* voice. No, this time she used her *"Dammit! I slept through the alarm! Get out of bed NOW!"* voice. The voice that sends adrenaline shock waves right through my body. The voice that makes me jump out of bed in the hopes that standing upright will make the noise stop. The voice that could wake the dead — although it didn't wake Shelley. Never does.

By the time I'd made my bed, washed my face and gotten dressed, Shelley had...well, Shelley had done nothing. *She* was still a lump under the covers. So Mom used her emergency back-up plan. She leaned over Shelley and said, "Get out of bed this instant, or I'm sending Edward in to wake you up." It worked like a charm. Always does.

4:00 a.m.

Teary goodbyes at the airport. Teary for Mom, anyway. Edward didn't have time for blubbering. *He* was too busy taking inventory of his stuff — again — to make sure he'd packed everything he could possibly need for an eight-hour flight. Frankly, I thought he'd packed enough for an 80-hour flight.

Shelley wasn't exactly choked up, either. She was too busy

checking out people's clothes and commenting on who should never have been allowed to dress themselves. Witty? Not really, considering how *she* looked. She'd been so groggy, and in such a screaming rush to get dressed, she'd put her t-shirt on inside out.

No, the only one crying was Mom, and as she pulled ratty tissues out of her purse, she fired off an unending stream of questions. And guess who was the only one listening to her? Right. Me.

"Monica, are you sure you have the traveler's checks?"

"Yes."

"And I gave you the number for the nurse's station, in case you need to reach me?"

"Yes."

"And you'll call as soon as you get to Grandma's so I'll know you're okay?"

"Yes."

"And you won't let any strange men get chummy with you on the plane?"

"Yes...I mean, No! *Mom!*"

Okay, so I wasn't exactly listening to her, either.

Suddenly, a loud grinding sound made Mom spin around. Edward was crouched down, leaning against the water fountain. He had his full-sized, battery-operated pencil sharpener clamped tightly between his knees, and he'd dumped his biggest pack of pencil crayons — there must have been 100 in the box — into a messy heap on the floor. He was sharpening them into razor-like points, then stuffing them into his carryon bag as fast as his scrawny little arms could move.

The three of us — me, Mom holding her mangled tissues, and the Fashion Goddess with her shirt tags sticking out — just stood there. Speechless. You have to understand, Edward does a lot of weird things — and I mean a *lot* of weird things. But this was bizarre, even for him. Edward never dumped anything. And he never *stuffed* anything. He sorted, he filed, he planned, he organized...he was only 10, but he was already Mr. Anal.

Suddenly, Mom leaned in close to me and lowered her voice. She looked almost...desperate.

"Listen," she said. "I know you really wanted to go to that science camp in August. And I know I said no. But you're the only one I can trust to make this work."

She glanced at Edward and Shelley, then leaned in even closer — we were almost nose-to-nose. "You get those two through this trip without something going wrong — and help me get Grandma into that old folk's home — and I'll sign you up for the whole month of August. I don't even care how much it costs."

My heart skipped a beat. This was my absolute dream — a month (a full month!) at a camp up north doing wacky science experiments with dozens of other science nerds. Four whole weeks without Edward and Shelley. Four whole weeks where I'd be surrounded by people just like me — where I'd feel like I belonged. I was in heaven.

5:00 a.m.

The flight attendants did their speech about what to do if the plane crashes (oddly, they never mentioned peeing your pants, which is what *I* would certainly do). Then the pilot announced that, although there would likely be turbulence, he was "looking forward to a pleasant flight." Then...well, then the plane took off.

No problem, right?

5:21 a.m.

Wrong. You know those little airplane barf bags they tell

you to use if you're going to be sick? *Not* roomy enough for someone who ate the Breakfast Special in the airport restaurant just before boarding.

"I feel like crud," Shelley muttered, as she slumped forward in her seat. "I think I'm gonna be sick again."

She *looked* like crud, too. Throwing up — loudly and dramatically, I'd like to add — had done nothing for her complexion.

"Well, you look fine," I said. It wasn't really a lie, if you think about it — "fine" is a vague term. And she probably would have looked worse if she'd been hit by a truck.

Edward didn't seem worried about the Incredible Barfing Sister — and the turbulence wasn't bothering him one bit, either. In fact, he seemed to be enjoying it.

"Do you like this one?" Edward asked. "It's a goat." Yes, Edward had made a goat — a tiny origami goat that was no bigger than a quarter. Although I'd cut out my own tongue before admitting it out loud, he wasn't just a dork — he was a fairly talented dork. His desk, his dresser, his bookshelf...his whole room was decorated with origami animals, and over the last few years he'd figured out how to make them smaller and smaller, using thin specialty paper plus tiny tweezers to hold the little scraps while he worked.

For the flight, Edward had picked a farm animal theme, and even Shelley stumbling over his legs to get to the washroom wasn't slowing him down for a second. He'd already made three tiny origami things — a horse, a duck and now a goat. The weird thing, though? His hands were kind of shaky, which really messing up his technique. Everything he'd made looked like a bloated cow.

"Looks nice, Edward — can you make a sheep, now?" I really didn't care if he made a sheep, a donkey or a two-headed sloth, as long as he stayed busy for the next eight hours.

Edward hunched over in his seat, his left leg jiggling nonstop as he worked frantically with his tiny square of paper. Another bloated cow was about to be born. It would keep him busy for 10 minutes, at least. But the jiggling leg thing was new — and it was getting old, fast.

8:00 a.m.

The turbulence hadn't stopped for three hours. That's 180 minutes. Or 10,800 seconds if you wanted to get really technical about it. And I did, quite frankly. Shelley had turned a weird pale gray color. And her hair was soaked with sweat and stuck to her head. And her breath...

"Ugh," she groaned. "I feel sick again."

"Maybe you should just stay in the bathroom for a while...till you feel better. You could take your toothbrush." Yes, I was hinting. And who wouldn't? She had the worst case of vomit breath ever — it was like an acid cloud rolling past my face every time she breathed.

Shelley made a gagging noise and lurched out of her seat. She crawled over me and Edward, then staggered down the aisle. Clearly, letting her have the window seat had been a mistake — but now no one was willing to trade with her, thanks to the too-small-barf-bag incident.

Everyone in the aisles lunged out of her way (word had spread that "the buxom girl had a weak stomach") so she made it to the bathroom in time. But without her toothbrush. Even industrial-strength mints weren't going to help me, now — unless I shoved them up my nose.

Five more hours — five long hours — and we'd be in England. Suddenly, Edward's leg jerked and he kicked me in the shin.

"What is *wrong* with you?" I asked.

"I don't know. I feel weird." He *said* it weird, too — a little too loud, a little too squeaky. Something *was* wrong with him. My stomach turned. Couldn't they fly the plane faster than this? If I could just hand him over to Grandma before whatever was about to go terribly wrong *went* wrong, I'd be off the hook.

Vomit Breath staggered back from the bathroom, fell over us and sank into her seat. She ripped open the foil package she'd been carrying, shook out a pill and choked it down.

"What did you just take?" I asked.

"I don't know...Gravol or something. The stewardess gave it to me."

"They're called flight attendants, now," Edward said. "You know, it's funny when you think about it...the first flight attendants were actually nurses...no men were allowed...and they were forced to retire at 32, couldn't get married or have kids, couldn't gain weight...then they got their own union and..."

Disaster check: Edward's voice — getting louder and faster. Left leg — getting bouncier. And were his arms actually *quivering*, now? They were. Help me.

8:05 a.m.

Our stewardess — excuse me, our flight attendant — appeared. "Ah, I see the Gravol is helping your sister," she said, brightly. No kidding. Shelley's head had flopped onto her right shoulder — the one closest to me, of course. Her eyes were half shut and her mouth was hanging open. She wasn't dead, that's for sure — she was snoring loudly and blasting me with vomit breath — but at least she wasn't going to throw up for a while.

"And your brother is, um..." She was still smiling, but now it was one of those fake smiles that you kind of know is going to disappear the instant you turn your back.

Edward. He was working feverishly on another bloated

cow. But sticking out of his ridiculously curly brown hair was every single origami animal he'd made in the last three hours. Cows — there must have been 20 of them — sticking out at every possible angle. Some had gotten crushed as he'd stuffed them into his hair — bloated cows who'd met their death in a sea of brown ringlets.

I was stunned, to say the least. Edward *never* let his origami get mangled — he still had the first ones he'd made when he was in 2nd grade (over 30 of them, glued to the underside of his bed so Mom couldn't throw them out). And now mangled cows were dangling out of his hair like barnyard confetti. Whatever was wrong with him, even Gravol wasn't going to help.

8:06 a.m.

Found out what was wrong with him.

"I feel a little weird," Edward said, as he squirmed around in his seat. "I shouldn't have drunk that coffee, I guess."

"That *what?*" Suddenly, it was all making sense. Terrible, sickening sense.

"Well...Mom had a lot of leftover coffee in the pot this morning, and she told me to dump it out while she packed the car," Edward said, trying to put on his best it's-not-my-fault face (and failing miserably, I'd like to add). "I thought I'd try it, you know. And it wasn't half-bad, once I added lots of milk and sugar." Now his arms were doing something funny — twitching, actually. Edward, the kid who's normally so hyper that he never stops moving, was high on caffeine.

This was too much — I needed help. I turned to Shelley and jabbed her. Hard.

"Ungh," she said, as her eyes rolled up in her head and a string of drool worked its way down her chin. If she moved any less, she'd have to be reclassified as a garden gnome.

"Look," I turned back to Edward, who was now rocking in his seat and humming. "If you can just stay calm for a couple more hours..."

Suddenly Edward's eyes shot open. "The bathroom beckons," he squeaked, as he raced down the aisle, bloated cows dancing in his hair.

The caffeine had kicked in — really kicked in. This trip could *not* get worse.

10:15 a.m.

Okay, so I was wrong. Now the Barfing Queen and the Diarrhea King were taking turns lunging for the bathroom. And when they were actually sitting in their seats they were both filling me in — loudly — about how they were going to die. Shelley, apparently, from dehydration. Edward from exploding intestines.

"Your intestines can't explode," I told him — and not for the first time, either.

"Listen to them gurgling!" he moaned. "Oh, what have I done? And my pulse...oh, my poor heart!" Edward had checked his pulse every five minutes since his first bout of diarrhea. He'd been transformed, in just two hours, into a full-blown hypochondriac.

11:10 a.m.

I was staring at Edward, watching the caffeine ooze from his pores, when our flight attendant's huge smile shot in front of my face. "Is everything okay, here?" she asked, in her happy voice.

I took a breath. Shelley's second dose of Gravol had knocked her out, again, so I was on my own. "No, we're *not* okay. My brother had a lot of caffeine this morning, and if I don't get him distracted, he's going to cause trouble."

Apparently, those were the magic words. Her huge smile froze in place, and for a moment, she didn't speak. She'd seen Edward's obsessive origami work. She'd caught him rearranging the beverage trolley so everything would be in alphabetical order. She'd answered his questions — his many, many questions — about where the toilet water goes, how the air gets circulated through the plane, and how the pillows and blankets get sanitized. She'd even shown him where she was stowing the garbage, when he started worrying that she might be pitching it right out a window.

Personally, I'd have rather stuck my head into a bag of live eels than spend three more hours with a *caffeinated* version of Edward — and, clearly, she felt the same way.

"What do you need?" she asked. "I'll do anything I can." Her happy voice had disappeared. This was her name-your-price voice.

"He loves to eat — if we keep feeding him, he may calm down," I said. "Or, at least, he won't be able to talk as much. And he'll be in his seat."

Buns, milk, juice, cheese and crackers, fruit cocktail, ice cream, cookies...I hadn't realized they had so much food on airplanes. And I hadn't realized Edward could eat so much, either.

Clearly, our flight attendant had sent out word that the kid with the hair cows was unstable, because every single attendant on the plane waltzed by at least once to bring a tasty offering to calm the Caffeine Gods. It was all Edward could do to keep up with them while still working on his origami, checking his pulse and occasionally sprinting to the bathroom.

12:00 p.m.

"Seriously, Monica, this has been the best day of my life! My *entire life!*" Edward said (making me wonder if we were even related). The avalanche of food had kept him out of trouble for almost two hours, but he was still too loud, too squeaky and too jittery...plus he had a weird eye twitch, now, and his muscles were so tense he was almost vibrating. His origami was suffering, too. He'd claimed the last one was a chicken, and had refused to talk to me for 20 minutes after I told him it looked more like road kill. Those were, as you can imagine, the best 20 minutes of the whole flight for me.

Suddenly, Edward sat bolt upright. "We're here! We're here!" he yelled, bouncing wildly in his seat.

He was right. We were circling the Heathrow airport in London. And for the first time in hours, I felt like I could finally breathe. Soon, we'd land, and I'd hand my drugged, vomit-soaked sister and hyper, caffeine-soaked brother over to Grandma Flo.

We hadn't seen Grandma in almost a year — and I'll tell you, I'd never looked forward to seeing someone as much as I was looking forward to seeing her.

12:58 p.m.

It took an eternity (okay, 19 minutes — but it *felt* like an eternity) to land. Then I had to find the exit, find the baggage claim area, find our suitcases...all the while dragging Shelley along behind me, and trying to stop Edward from racing ahead. Somehow, I even managed to get my watch changed — it was almost 6 p.m. England time. The worst day of my life was, thankfully, almost over. And I was going to be rewarded very soon with four weeks of science camp bliss.

We turned the last corner, and there they were — hordes and hordes of people waiting to pick up passengers. And somewhere in there was our Grandma Flo, who was going to take over for me and make life calm again...make life *normal* again.

Suddenly, Edward froze — mouth hanging open, but strangely silent. And Shelley...she was frozen right beside him, eyes so wide she looked like she'd been electrocuted.

They were staring into the crowd. Staring at a lady who was waving wildly at us. A short, gray-haired old lady wearing bright red leather pants, bright red boots, and a blindingly white T-shirt that said (in bright red letters that stretched right across her massive breasts), "*Welcome to Titty Ho!*"

It was Grandma Flo.

Chapter 3

Flaming Hair And Public Peeing

I don't actually remember handing over my two poisoned siblings to Grandma — she must have seen my beaten expression and just taken over. And within minutes, we'd escaped that crowded airport and settled comfortably into the back of a cab.

"This is fabulous!" Edward squealed, as we raced through a yellow light.

I stifled a scream. Not because the light was yellow, mind you — turns out that in England, traffic lights turn yellow before they turn green. It means "time to get moving," not "time to hit the brakes," like it does here.

No, I stifled a scream because we were driving on the *wrong side of the road*. Even if I lived in England the rest of my life, I'd never get used to the fact that they drive on the wrong side of the road.

Whack! Ouch. We'd turned left again. And every time we turned left, my head smacked into the window beside me. Smacked it *hard*, too. The taxi driver clearly didn't believe in using the brakes — not even when he was going around corners.

Think I'm exaggerating? Well, picture this: Shelley's open purse had hit the floor when we swerved out of the airport parking lot — lip gloss, eye liner, mascara, hair clips...it all went flying. And she hadn't made any attempt to pick up her stuff. Why? Because she was too busy hanging onto the door handle with one hand, and Edward's arm with the other. The Cosmetics Queen was so busy trying to stay upright, she'd abandoned her beauty products. *That's* how fast we were going.

"This is fabulous!" Edward squealed. Again. Clearly, I'd picked the wrong seat. I'd stuck Edward between me and Shelley so I could get a break from Vomit Breath. But now *he* was bouncing around between us like a cushioned tennis ball, while *I* was bouncing off a thick sheet of window glass.

Whack! Another left. A lip liner rolled past my feet.

"So, did you like your grammy's shirt, Monica?" the taxi driver asked. He was grinning over his shoulder, and I'm only mentioning this because he was missing a few teeth. A lot of teeth, actually — he had about four on the top and four on the bottom. He looked like a gerbil.

"Um...I...well..." Yes, that was me. The Queen of Good Grammar. In June, I had the highest mark in English. Now it was July, and I couldn't answer a simple yes-or-no question.

He burst out laughing. "You know her shirt's a joke, right? Titty Ho is the name of a street in Raunds — a town about half an hour from your grammy's house. I got her that shirt so she could bug your Auntie Gay!"

I looked at Grandma — she was giggling and nodding. Her chins (she had two) were jiggling like mad.

"Clyde's my neighbor," she said, pointing at the gerbil in the front seat. Then she leaned forward and whispered, "He's a silly old goat, but very kind — he traded shifts with another bloke so he could give us a lift home from the airport."

Then she sat back, straightened her shirt so the words "Titty Ho" were back over her...well, you know...and patted her shiny red pants. "Your Auntie Gay hates leather, too — she'll only wear the hides of freshly-slaughtered polyesters," Grandma said. "That's why I bought these pants!"

Whack! Another left. Another head injury. I kicked the lip liner and a couple of tampons back to Shelley's side of the cab.

The toothless one called out from the front seat, "Your grammy's the life of the neighborhood, I'll tell you!"

"Grandma? The life of...what do you mean?" Shelley asked, as she tried to reach a tampon with her foot. No luck. That cab was *huge*. It was taller, wider and longer than a normal car. There was room for six people in the back — three facing forward and three facing backward. Grandma was sitting on the backward-facing seat, and there was so much room between us that I doubt I could have reached her, even if I'd stuck my leg all the way out. There were loads of these taxis in England, Grandma had said — although I doubted the others were filled with roaming tampons and 14-year-olds with concussions.

"Grandma, why are you moving into an old folk's home?" Edward asked. Just like that, he dropped a verbal bomb. No warning, no hinting, no chance to shut him up. That was Edward for you.

Grandma frowned and crossed her arms in front of her chest (no small task, I'll tell you). "I'm not going into a care home, no matter what that crusty old bat thinks." The "crusty old bat" was Auntie Gay, Grandma's youngest sister — which makes her our *Great* Aunt, I suppose.

"In England, the government makes you sell your home and give them every scrap of your money as payment for taking care of you," she said. "It's robbery! And I can take care of myself just fine, don't you think?"

I tried to not look at her Titty Ho shirt. "Yes you can, Grandma." I didn't mean it, of course, but I didn't want to hurt her feelings, either. If Mom said Grandma needed to go into a senior's home, then that was that. Besides, Grandma's outfit was, well, wow. Obviously, Grandma was going senile or something.

"Then why does Auntie Gay think you need to go into a home? What's wrong?" Edward asked. I gave him my look. My *Mom told us to not talk about this, so stop before I have to kill you*, look. But, as usual, Edward was wrapped up in his own little dream world and wasn't noticing my glares.

"Because she's lost her mind," bellowed the gerbil, making all four of us jump. "It's that bloody wedding — you'd think she was the Queen the way she's carrying on. She's got it in her head that your grammy's lost her marbles, but *she's* the one who's missing a few — that's what *I* think!"

Grandma nodded as she kicked a tube of mascara back toward Shelley's abandoned purse. "Don't you listen to her silliness," she said. "I'm perfectly fine on my own, and I'm not moving anywhere."

Suddenly, the tires squealed. We were home — at least, the place we'd be calling home for the next nine days.

I'd seen pictures of Grandma's house (she brought photos each summer so we could see her gardens) but nothing could have prepared me for the real thing. Grandma lived in a tiny, 450-year-old gray stone cottage with a thatched roof — the type of roof that looks like straw that's been combed down neatly and covered with chicken wire. The yard was full of flowering trees and shrubs, and there was a vine-covered stone fence — a stone fence as old as the house — wrapped around the garden.

"This is fabulous!" Edward squealed, as he scrambled over my legs to get out. Shelley practically knocked me over trying to get out next — relieved, no doubt, to be on solid ground. As

Clyde raced off down the road, I hurried up the stone walkway to join them.

I hated to admit it, but Edward was right. This *was* fabulous. Everything was perfect — even the door looked freshly painted and the lawn was freshly mowed. Why did Mom think Grandma couldn't take care of herself, I wondered, as I stepped into her quaint little house.

Oh.

Edward and Shelley were standing side-by-side in the entryway. Frozen. Silent.

Why? Well, picture Shelley's half of our bedroom — her messy, cluttered, disorganized half of our bedroom. And picture that mess exploding inside a small, 450-year-old house. Sound like a disaster? This was worse. Much, much worse.

I could see some of the basics — we were standing in the living room, there was a small kitchen on the right, a bedroom and bathroom on the left and narrow, wooden stairs going up the back wall to the attic.

But what color were the walls? The floor? The furniture? I couldn't tell you, because every surface — every single surface — was covered with...stuff. Dishes, jars, boxes, clothes, blankets, pictures, shoes, books, bottles, newspapers...and staring at us across this messy, cluttered space was the biggest, blackest, hairiest dog I'd ever seen in my life.

"It's a dog!" Shelley shrieked (she really did have a great grasp of the obvious).

"You've seen pictures of Fred," Grandma laughed. "Try not to startle him. He's 12, now, and he's having a little trouble with his bladder." I took a step back as Fred lumbered slowly toward us. Fred's a Newfoundland — a Newfie — and he weighs about 150 pounds. And if there was one thing I did *not* want to startle, it was a 150-pound dog with a bladder control problem. He was a walking urine bomb.

"This is fabulous!" Edward squealed, as he raced across the room to give Fred a big hug. Then, graceful as a gazelle, Edward leapt over a stack of books, tripped on a chair and fell flat on his face, sending cats — four of them, at least — scattering across the room.

"That's Grumpy and that's Bashful." Grandma pointed at the two cats scrambling under the couch. "And those two are Happy and Sleepy." Happy and Sleepy had leapt onto the kitchen counter — and with their backs arched, fur standing up straight, ears pulled back and tails flicking madly, they didn't look happy *or* sleepy.

"I thought you only had two cats," Shelley said. "And...I thought they were called Mortimer and Rufus."

"Well, yes...but five more showed up last winter and I didn't have the heart to send them off, so I changed their names to the seven dwarfs." Grandma pulled bags and boxes off the couch...and heaped them onto the coffee table. "Besides, it really doesn't matter what you name cats — they never come when you call them."

"Go unpack," she added, nodding toward the stairs. "Then you can relax while I make tea."

I stared at the couch. I could sit on it, I suppose, but I'd never be able to relax. It was coated with enough stray pet hair to make another cat — the long-lost eighth dwarf. And the dog that had produced most of this mess was now sprawled across half the couch, keeping a wary eye on Edward, who was bouncing around the room, catching and petting one irritated cat after another.

I was about to head up the stairs when something caught my eye — something white poking out between the couch cushions. I stuck my hand in — which, quite frankly, I thought was very brave — and pulled out...a bra. Grandma's bra, I'm guessing. But more to the point, it was the *biggest* bra I'd ever seen. I stood there in awe — half-jealous, half-horrified. It was the size of two grocery bags stuck together. If I'd pulled one of the cups over my head, it would have hung all the way down to my shoulders. I didn't try, of course, so I'm only guessing.

"Your Auntie Gay's invited 292 people to this wedding — can you imagine?" Grandma called from the kitchen. "She's finally conned some poor man into marrying her, and she thinks 292 people should buy her gifts — it's ridiculous!"

Ridiculous, yes. Which was how I was going to feel if I got caught with the world's biggest bra in my hand. I quickly stuffed it back between the cushions and headed for the stairs.

"It does seem like a lot, Grandma," I agreed, as I grabbed Edward and dragged him along with me. There was no telling what that kid would do if he was left unsupervised with a massive bra — but I was pretty sure it would involve at least two snarly cats.

Shelley was already upstairs, walking around with a curling iron in her hand and a bewildered look on her face. Clearly, she didn't think she looked perfect enough for an evening at Grandma's house. And, clearly, there were no electrical outlets in sight.

The attic was actually one big room with very low windows that were right at floor level — I had to squat down to see out. And the room had a sloped ceiling that was so low, Shelley had to duck a bit when she walked. It had been set up as a guest room — four beds lined the longest wall — but, like downstairs, every single surface was heaped with dusty, unused...stuff.

"Found one!" Shelley yelled, as she pulled boxes away from the wall and plugged her curling iron into the old-fashioned outlet.

"We definitely need to get Grandma into an old folk's home," I said.

"I *knew* you'd say that," Shelley muttered, as she pulled a crate of books and a broken chair off her bed. "If someone isn't perfectly organized and perfectly clean and perfectly...perfect, *you* think something's wrong with them." Shelley rubbed her nose, trying to stop herself from sneezing as dust billowed up around her face.

"Plus, there's your stupid science camp — better to dump Grandma into a home than miss out on that," she added, sarcastically.

Shelley must have heard what Mom had said at the airport. But now she was twisting it around, trying to make me sound bad, which was completely unfair.

"Have you *looked* at this place?" I asked, waving my arms randomly (you really didn't need to look at anything in particular to make this point). "I don't think she's cleaned in 20 years. How can she live like this? It's just not healthy!"

"A little dirt never hurt anyone." Shelley picked the dust bunnies off her pants. "And if you weren't so anal, you'd see that she's doing just fine."

Suddenly, the cat Edward was holding heard the call of the wild and went berserk. Edward — who's a big fan of skin, and gets quite squeamish when he loses chunks of his — dropped the ball of fury, stumbled sideways and did his gazelle thing again, landing face-first on the floor.

"Do you see what I mean?" I said, pointing at Edward. "This is *not* a safe place to live."

"You're an idiot." Shelley turned her back to me and started curling her bangs. That's her idea of how to win an argument — toss out a lame insult and then turn away.

"Oh, my...um, Monica, you might be right." It was Edward. Still sprawled across the floor, he now had a perfect view through the floor-height window that looked out into the back yard.

"Oh no...oh NO!" Shelley screamed, as she staggered backward, shaking her head wildly from side to side.

"Monica!" Edward yelled. "Grandma's peeing in her garden!"

"Monica!" Shelley screamed. "*My hair's on fire!*"

And, indeed, it was.

Chapter 4

That Really Hurt

Ever been in a situation where you wanted to run in two different directions at the same time, and ended up frozen on the spot, instead? Well, I *wish* that's what had happened next — it would have been a lot less painful. Truth is, I really didn't want to see Grandma peeing in her garden — she was still wearing her tight leather pants, so this wasn't a simple "hike up your skirt and go" kind of event.

So I ran straight for Shelley to find out why there was smoke billowing out of her hair. And that's when I slammed into Edward, who'd leapt off the floor and was sprinting toward the window (the little chicken was trying to avoid dealing with Shelley). We ricocheted off each other and Edward landed on the bare wood floor, while *I* crashed into a pile of old, dusty boxes. I was lying there trying to recall the names of all the bones I'd probably broken, when Shelley turned into a diva. Again.

"Monica! Get over here and help me!" she shrieked, as she whacked her smoking head with a pillow. I limped across the room, rubbing my leg. There was no point in rushing, anymore. True, there were still a few wisps of smoke coming from her head, but you could barely see them through the cloud of dust (that pillow must have been 100 years old). She wasn't exactly a human blowtorch or anything — more like a smoking dust bunny.

"What does it look like? Tell me!" Shelley wailed, as she poked away at her charred hair.

"It looks like you've been electrocuted," I said. And it kind of did, actually. She'd only burned one chunk of hair, but it was a big chunk, and it was right at the front. Now, instead of lying neatly over her forehead, her bangs were standing straight up and looking...crispy. There was really no other word to describe them.

"Okay, Grandma's pants are up." Edward said — sounding oddly businesslike — as he scrambled down the stairs. I didn't want to be in the room when Shelley found a mirror and saw what she looked like, so I limped downstairs after him.

We squeezed out the back door at pretty much the same time, and there she was. Our grandma. Standing there in her Titty Ho shirt and bright red pants, casually filling up a bunch of plastic bowls from a big bag of cat food and acting like nothing was wrong. Acting like she hadn't just pulled her pants down in front of, well, potentially the entire neighborhood. Acting like she didn't need to be put in a senior's home — which she clearly did.

Edward and I just stood there watching her. Silent. I mean, really, what do you say to someone who's done something that nutty? Something that weird? Something that bizarre?

"Why'd you pee in your garden?" Edward asked. Okay, so that was one option.

"It keeps the stray cats out of my flower beds," Grandma

said, as she set a bowl of cat food beside her lilac bush. "If they smell urine, they assume the area's been marked by another cat and they leave it alone."

"Um...maybe if you stopped feeding them, they'd stop hanging around," I said. No, I wasn't being snotty — you were probably thinking the same thing.

"Oh, don't be silly! They need to eat," she replied. "If I didn't feed the little things, they'd...oh, *bloody hell!*" She grabbed the broom that was leaning against her picnic table and smacked one of her big shrubs. Flower petals exploded into the air as a cat — the ugliest, skinniest cat I'd ever seen — raced across the lawn as if it had been fired from a cannon.

"Shoo, you miserable old thing!" she yelled. "No pooping in my bushes!"

Suddenly, a wail drifted from the house.

"Noooooooo..." It was Shelley. Apparently, she'd found a mirror.

I gave Grandma a quick rundown of the flaming hair incident as we scuttled inside. Good thing, too, because it wasn't a pretty sight. Shelley was standing in Grandma's bathroom staring in the mirror, a brush dangling from one hand, curling iron dangling from the other, bangs standing straight up.

Grandma's eyebrows slid halfway up her forehead and she pursed her lips together extra hard (the way people do when they're trying to look serious, even though they're about to pee themselves laughing). Then, quick as anything, she sprang into action.

"No worries, dear, we'll have your fringe fixed in no time." Grandma carefully clipped off the blackest pieces of Shelley's bangs — which was pretty much all of them.

"A fringe is your bangs," Edward whispered, as he poked me, hard, with his bony little elbow. "That's what they call them in England."

"I don't understand," Shelley wailed. "I used an adapter, just like the guide book said."

"Adapters just let you plug American appliances into European wall sockets," Grandma said. "The problem is that our voltage is 240 and yours is 110 — your iron overheated because way too much electricity went through it."

"But how will I curl my bangs if I can't use my curling iron?" Shelley asked.

"Um...I don't think you'll need to worry about that for a little while, dear." Grandma was doing her pursed-lip thing again, as she rearranged what was left of Shelley's bangs. "A few hair grips and you'll look just beautiful — I think you look better without a fringe, anyway."

Another painful elbow jab. "Hair grips are bobby pins," Edward whispered. "That's what they call them in England." Getting him that book on British culture had seemed like a great idea last winter. Now, I wasn't so sure.

I don't know how long we would have stood there — admiring the spot where Shelley's bangs used to be — but the loud slam of a car door brought us back to reality.

"Ugh, I bet that's the crusty old bat — the *Queen* of Old Warden," Grandma muttered, as she swept Shelley's charred hair into the sink (or, at least, in the general direction of the sink — Grandma certainly wasn't a clean freak).

Auntie Gay didn't even knock. She just threw the door open and swept into the living room. She made quite an entrance, too, thanks to her frilly pink dress and matching hat, shoes and purse — it was kind of like looking at a big gob of pink cotton candy with a wrinkled old lady's face peeking out of it.

She had one of those flashy, just-bleached-my-teeth smiles pasted on her face, too — until she stepped in the puddle of pee Fred had left by the door.

"Flo! That disgusting dog of yours." Auntie Gay scowled at Grandma as she wiped her cotton candy shoe off on the mat. "I can't believe you still keep that thing."

Grandma sighed. "Gay, shut your cake hole and say hello to your relatives."

Now, I've never been very good at small talk. Plus Grandma was hovering by the door, mopping up dog pee and making silly faces behind Auntie Gay's back. So it was a bit awkward, as you can imagine. Then Edward and Grandma made it infinitely worse by bailing on me and sneaking out into the garden.

"Finally, time for some girl talk," Auntie Gay said, as she wobbled over to the couch (some people really shouldn't wear high heels).

"Clearly, my poor sister needs to go into a care home, don't you agree?" Auntie Gay asked. Shelley gave me a death glare as she stomped into the bathroom.

I peeked out the window. Grandma and Edward had wrapped themselves in sheets they'd pulled off the clothesline, and they were walking behind Fred, waving their arms and pretending they were in some sort of parade.

"It would probably be best, yes," I said.

Slam! Ah, yes, Shelley. She wasn't going to get involved in the conversation, but she *was* going to make her opinion known by slamming the drawers of the old dresser in Grandma's bathroom.

"Well, we simply have to convince her that it's the right thing to do." Auntie Gay rearranged the ruffles on her dress. "And I bet she'd listen to you two — you're such mature girls."

Slam! One of us was, anyway.

"Mom never mentioned that Grandma's house looked like...this. I don't understand why she didn't warn us."

"Remember, dear, your mom hasn't been to England in four years — not since your Grandma started making summer trips to your place. I'm sure she has no idea how bad it is now — she'll be horrified, don't you think?"

Slam! She was going to be horrified by the condition of Grandma's antique dresser — no question about that.

I snuck another peek out the window. Grandma and Edward were still doing the parade thing, but now they had flowers hanging out of their hair, Fred was draped in sheets, and they'd picked up a couple of cats along the way. It was now a hippie parade — with hairballs.

Auntie Gay turned to see what I was looking at, then sniffed in disgust. "Honestly, Monica, those two are a pair of right nutters," she said. "You can see where he gets it, can't you?"

Well, I know this sounds weird, but that kind of ticked me off. I know Edward's a pain, but he's my brother. *I'm* the one who gets to insult him, not a virtual stranger wearing urine-soaked shoes.

"Well, he's a bit...different, but that doesn't mean there's something actually *wrong* with him," I blurted out.

Auntie Gay stood up and put on her best ticked-off face (clearly, this was a face she used a lot). "I'll be back shortly to get this wrapped up," she said, as she wobbled out the front door. "Just wait until your mother sees this mess."

When she'd finally stuffed her dress into the car and raced away from the curb, I headed out to the garden to see what Edward and Grandma were doing. Shelley followed. Apparently, she'd run out of drawers to break.

Fred was sprawled out in the middle of the lawn, fast asleep. The parade cats had been released, and they were pacing along the top of Grandma's stone fence — trying to decide which bush to pee in, no doubt. And Grandma and Edward? They were sitting quietly at the picnic table, playing chess.

"Checkmate!" Grandma said, as she sat back and rearranged the flowers in her hair.

Edward stared at the board, bewildered, then dropped his head into his hands and groaned.

Shelley turned and stared right at me — almost daring me to make eye contact. *No one* played chess with Edward and won. Mom and I had been playing against him since the little brat was seven, and neither of us had ever won a game against him. *Ever.*

"There's nothing wrong with Grandma's brain," Shelley hissed.

"She's disorganized and her house is a dump — it's wrong to live like this," I hissed back.

We stood there, kind of scowling at each other, waiting to see who'd speak next. I was so sick of Shelley, I couldn't *wait* to get away from her in August. I really couldn't.

Suddenly, Grandma clapped her hands and leapt out of her chair. "Time for tea! You kiddos must be exhausted!"

You know, I'd been so busy that I hadn't noticed, but I really *was* tired — so tired that I didn't even want a cup of tea. So while Edward followed Grandma around the kitchen trying to con her into a rematch, and while Shelley stood in the bathroom trying to will her bangs to re-grow, I stumbled upstairs to go to bed.

Sound simple? Not a chance. Shelley had already claimed the bed with the broken chair and crate of books on it. And Edward had dumped his suitcase on the one with lots of extra blankets (about 20 of them, if the height of the bed was any indication).

My choices were either the bed by the window, which was heaped with dusty old boxes, or the one by the stairs, which had a big indent in the middle — an indent full of black hair. It was probably from one of Grandma's cats. But it could have been from a stray dog, a skunk, or a rabid raccoon...there was really no way to tell until the hairs' owner crawled back onto the bed in the middle of the night. I sighed and started pulling boxes off the bed by the window.

And it wouldn't have taken me very long, either — if I hadn't fallen into the hole.

Chapter 5

The Toothbrush Tragedy

If you had asked me ahead of time how I'd react if I suddenly fell into a hole, I'd have guessed that I'd throw my arms out to break my fall. Sounds logical, but that wasn't what happened.

No, when I stepped on the plywood cover and broke it, my left leg plunged through the round hole in the floor, while my arms just kind of wind-milled around above my head like a couple of startled birds. I did nothing to break my fall — nothing at all — so it's no surprise that I ended up jammed in the hole right up to my crotch (which was surprisingly painful), with my left leg dangling straight down into the living room, and my right leg stuck straight out in front of me on the bedroom floor.

Ballerinas spend years trying to perfect poses like that, and I'd pulled it off in a matter of seconds — although there was a pretty good chance I'd never be able to have kids. You might be assuming this was the dumbest thing I did the entire trip. You'd be wrong, but I'll get to that later.

"Goodness!" I heard Grandma say, as she and Shelley pounded up the stairs.

Edward didn't follow them. Instead, he raced into the living room and started discussing this startling turn of events with my leg. He explained to my leg why there was such a big hole in the floor (the nutty man who owned the house 60 years ago had wanted more heat from the fireplace to get upstairs) and he told my leg how frequently amputations occur during serious home accidents (very frequently). He said some other stuff, too, but I wasn't really listening — my leg was too busy swinging around wildly, trying to kick him in the head. I really needed a break from him. I really really *really* needed to go to that science camp.

After pulling me out of the hole, Grandma unearthed her first aid kit. It turned out to be almost as old as she was — which is 77, in case I forgot to mention it earlier. The rusty old box was filled with TCP (an antiseptic kind of like rubbing alcohol), surgical tape — which was useless, since there was no gauze — and, oddly, a bottle of brandy. I pretended my leg felt fine and crawled into bed. The truth is, it felt awful, but there wasn't much point in dwelling on it.

Nothing deadens brain cells faster than six hours of crappy sleep. And thanks to the seven dwarfs, that's exactly what I got. Grumpy, Dopey, Happy, Sneezy, Doc...one by one, they jumped onto the bed and tried to sleep on my head. And, one by one, I pitched them onto the floor.

I'd finally drifted off to sleep when I felt a breeze on my face. A warm breeze. A warm, nasty-smelling breeze. I forced my eyes open, only to discover another set of eyes staring right back at me. It was Fred.

He was standing beside the bed with his head resting on my pillow, his nose almost touching mine and a thick line of drool coming from his mouth. As soon as he saw my eyes open, he snorted and — in a surprising burst of energy for a dog his age — hopped up onto the bed and gave me a shove. Next thing I knew, I was lying on the floor, with Fred sprawled across the bed, calmly staring at me. Fred, I discovered, was a serious bed hog.

I stood up slowly and checked my body for damage. And much as I would have loved to whine for a few minutes, there really wasn't much to report. My left leg was bruised from falling into the boxes, and skinned from falling into the hole. Other than that, I felt fine. That is, until I turned the wrong way and whacked my head on the low, sloped ceiling.

Thonk. Okay, so I wasn't exactly awake. Sleep deprivation and jet lag make a nasty combination. I was going to have to be careful, or I'd end up walking in front of a bus.

I tiptoed past Shelley, who was still asleep. She was quite a sight, too, lying on her back, mouth hanging open, charred bangs sticking straight up like little radio antennae. Her hairstyle wouldn't be showing up on the cover of *Seventeen* any time soon.

And Edward? His bed was a mess — it looked like he'd used all 20 blankets — but he was nowhere to be seen.

"Oh, nooooooo…" Edward's agonized wail drifted up the stairs. Clearly, he'd conned Grandma into an early-morning chess game. And clearly he'd lost. Again.

"Stupid people aren't the only ones who can be selfish, you know." Great. Shelley had woken up enough to make my life miserable again. She was thrashing around like a cat in a bag, trying to get out from under all the blankets. "You saw her play chess — you know there's nothing wrong with her brain. If it weren't for that science camp you want to go to, you'd be trying to stop this."

"That's not true," I said, staring out one of the low, dusty, greasy windows. "Nobody should live like this."

"Nobody should *judge* people who live like this," Shelley said.

I couldn't think of a snotty retort, so I grabbed my toothbrush and stumbled down the stairs, leaning against the wall for support (my knees still had the morning wobbles). And there they were, Grandma and Edward, hunched over a chessboard at the kitchen table. Edward was wearing a brand-new pair of Superman pajamas, and Grandma was wearing...Superman pajamas? My grandma — who had, quite possibly, the biggest breasts in the world — was wearing PJ's that came with a floor-length cape.

"Good morning, Monica," Grandma said, as she refilled her teacup. "I sewed Edward some jimjams so we could match when you came for your visit."

"Jimjams are pajamas," Edward said. "That's what they call them in England."

"I'm...I'm going to brush my teeth." I veered off toward the bathroom. I wasn't ready to talk, yet — especially not to two super heroes eating chocolate chip cookies and playing chess at 7 a.m.

Grandma looked at Edward and raised her eyebrows. "Monica brushes *before* breakfast?" she asked.

He shook his head and put on that worldly, know-it-all look that I hate. "That's just the tip of the iceberg," the little snot said, as he rearranged his cape. "You'd be amazed at how anal she is." I didn't have the energy to kill him, so I sent out a wish that he'd lose his next chess match — which would be pretty much the same thing, as far as Edward was concerned.

I stepped carefully into the bathroom. I hate bathrooms. Even at the best of times, they're not particularly sanitary. And this was not the best of times, either. I don't have the stomach to describe it, so just picture "grimy, slimy and crammed with stuff" and you'll have it nailed.

I was still standing at the counter, looking for a safe spot to hide my toothbrush so toilet water couldn't rain down on it, when Fred shoved the door open with his massive head. Then, acting like it was really no big deal, he lumbered over to the toilet, used his big bed-stealing snout to lift the lid, and started...*drinking*! The dog that had breathed all over my face and drooled on my bed was drinking toilet water. I was going to have to burn my pillow.

I carefully pushed his head away from the bowl with my leg and dropped the lid down (using my foot, of course — toilet seats are very unsanitary). He just looked at me, lifted the lid and started drinking again. So I pushed his head away and closed the lid. So he...okay, I won't bore you with the details. Here's the short version: I had a battle of wills with a 12-year-old incontinent dog...and lost.

When I realized it was hopeless, I wrapped my toothbrush in a clean facecloth and tucked it behind the food processor that was sitting beside the sink (no, I have no idea why it was there). It wasn't an ideal spot to store a toothbrush, but it would have to do, because chances were slim any of the drawers had room for my stuff — and I wasn't about to open them to find out, either.

I'd just stepped out of the bathroom — the picture of glamour in my rumpled pajamas, unwashed face and award-winning bed-head — when the front door flew open. It was Auntie Gay, who clearly did not believe in knocking.

It was almost painful to look at her. She was wearing a bright, eye-searing yellow skirt and blouse (covered with ruffles, of course). And I wasn't the slightest bit surprised to see that her shoes, purse and big flowery hat all matched her outfit perfectly. She looked like she'd been attacked by a mob of angry daffodils. I was starting to wonder what her wedding dress was going to look like.

She was carrying a big paper shopping bag and — without even stopping to say hello — she stomped over to the kitchen table and poured out...vitamins. There must have been eight different bottles.

"I'm stocking you up before the wedding, because I will *not* have time to fuss with things like this when I'm on my honeymoon," Auntie Gay said. "Now, you need to take one of each every day — and, for Heaven's sake, take them with food, so you'll absorb them properly."

"Don't know why you bother with those silly things," Grandma said, as she nibbled a cookie and watched Edward set up the chessboard for his next round of torture. "You know I'm just going to take random fistfuls whenever I think about it."

Auntie Gay's cheeks turned a pinkish-red color — which would have looked nice, except it kind of clashed with the daffodil theme.

"You are so difficult!" she said. "Your diet is terrible and you drink too much. You need to take vitamins, or you'll be dead — you just watch."

"Logically, I will not be able to watch *anything* once I'm dead." Grandma moved her first pawn. "And taking them in random fistfuls whenever I remember has been working just fine for me."

"Oh, you are so...so...aaarrrggghhh! Take the damned vitamins you stubborn old cow!" Auntie Gay stormed out, slamming the door quite dramatically behind her.

Grandma ate the last of her cookie as her sister sped off down the road. Then she opened the vitamin bottles and carefully shook one pill out of each.

"Grandma!" Edward said. "Why did you tell Auntie Gay you take random fistfuls? You're just making her mad."

Grandma frowned. "She's a bossy old witch and a control

freak, and she thinks that just because she's younger, she can run my life," Grandma said.

"Younger sisters are idiots," Shelley muttered, as she slowly wobbled down the stairs, leaning against the wall for support. Her eyes were puffy and red, her cheeks were blotted with mascara and her hair was sticking out at every possible angle. Shelley wasn't much of a morning person. She wasn't much of an afternoon or evening person, either, but that's another matter.

"Checkmate!" Grandma reached for another cookie as Edward clutched his chest and toppled — in true Drama Queen style — off his chair. Cats scattered as he lay there, moaning.

"I've got a good idea," said Shelley, who'd never had a good idea in her life. "Auntie Gay's figuring Mom will want to put you in a home once she sees this place. But if we tidy up before she gets here, Mom would see that you *can* take care of yourself."

I glared at Shelley as hard as I could, willing her to make eye contact so I could burn a hole through her head. No luck. She'd made it down the stairs, but now she was sitting on the floor with her eyes half-closed and her legs sprawled out in front of her.

A smile spread across Grandma's face. "Sounds fun," she said, as she sat back and rested her teacup on her breasts. "It shouldn't take more than a couple of hours to hoover this place out."

Horrified, I looked around the room — at the boxes, the bags, the dirt, the bedlam — as Edward slowly climbed back onto his chair.

"Hoover," he said weakly, "means vacuum. That's what these sneaky British chess fiends call it."

Suddenly, Shelley perked up and smiled.

"Hey, Monica!"

"What?" I was suspicious, as you can imagine — Shelley never smiled before noon.

She pointed at Fred, who was sprawled across the living room rug, chewing something.

"Isn't that your toothbrush?"

Chapter 6

Rutabaga Is Not A Vegetable

Sadly, it *was* my toothbrush. And even after scrubbing it with the hand sanitizer I always kept in my purse, I couldn't make myself use it. I just knew that somewhere, buried deep between those bristles, was a microscopic gob of dog slobber. So into the garbage it went — and out came a replacement toothbrush from Grandma's storage closet.

"I'd meant it for Edward," she said, apologetically.

"That's okay, Grandma." I wrapped my new Daffy Duck toothbrush in a clean cloth and stuck it in my back pocket. And it really *was* okay. I wouldn't have cared if there'd been an entire flock of cartoon characters glued to the stupid thing — Daffy had never been in Fred's mouth, and that was all that really mattered.

I'd gotten dressed, made my bed, brushed my hair and washed my face — and Shelley had just woken up enough to realize that she was sitting at the bottom of the stairs in her pajamas — when Grandma called us for breakfast.

One look at the table told me why Auntie Gay was in such a snit about vitamins. Toast, eggs, fruit...there were a lot of things that wouldn't have surprised me at 8 a.m. But a cake covered with blazing candles, a huge carton of ice cream and party hats? Okay, I was surprised.

"We're having an *un*birthday party!" Grandma said, as she strapped on her party hat. "I don't know anyone who has a birthday this month, so we're going to celebrate *No One's* birthday!"

I bet you're thinking I felt weird about putting on a party hat, singing happy birthday to No One and then eating a huge plate of cake and ice cream first thing in the morning. Well, think again. I love sugar. I live for sugar. If I ever find out I'm going to be dead in a week, all I'll eat — for seven days straight — is sugar.

I ate so much I thought I was going to barf. Edward ate so much that he *did* barf (Edward's never been very good at figuring out when he's full).

Shelley pretty much just sat there looking ridiculous — she'd forgotten to brush her hair, so it poked out from under her party hat like matted straw. She picked at her cake — and picked at me, as well.

"You're just trying to make everything go your way so you can get your stupid trip," she whispered.

"That's not fair — you know this isn't a healthy way to live," I whispered back. "And, besides, why do *you* care?"

"Because *I* think it's more important for Grandma to be happy than for you to get what you want." Shelley stared at me coldly. My stomach tightened. Probably too much cake.

"But *you're* trying to get your way, too — what's the difference?"

"The difference," Shelley said, staring at me coldly, "is that

I'm trying to help Grandma get what *she* wants — *you're* trying to get what *you* want."

I knew it wasn't true. But when Shelley said it like that, it sounded brutal.

I shook my head hard, then turned back to Grandma. She was busy explaining to Edward why this was actually a very healthy breakfast. "The cake is made with eggs, and this is strawberry ice cream, so it contains dairy *and* fruit."

She was also quick to explain why we shouldn't mention this to Auntie Gay. "She'd kill me," Grandma said, as she piled a second helping onto Fred's plate.

Cleanup was quick, since Grandma's idea of doing the dishes was to stack them in the sink on top of the other dirty dishes. And that left me staring, silent and numb, at the job that faced us. The place was packed — practically floor to ceiling — with junk. Clearly, this was going to be impossible.

"Right. I'll be back in a jiffy," Grandma said, as she stomped out the front door. "You three best get started, because the old cow will be back tonight and you're wanting to surprise her, right?"

Shelley swung around to face me, cake crumbs still clinging to her pajamas, party hat slipping off the side of her head. "Grandma thinks we can clean this place in one day?"

For a few seconds, I just stared at her. This was a whole new level of dumb for Shelley. "This was *your* idea!" I said.

"Well, yes, but I didn't think...I figured we'd have more time to...I didn't mean...I..." Cripes. It was the beginning of a hellishly long day of cleaning and organizing, and I had to spend it with a sister who couldn't put a simple sentence together. Oh, and a brother who never shut up.

"Look what I found!" Edward yelled. He held up a book, gave it a shake and out fluttered...money. "It's £35 — that's about $56 in our money!" He flapped the bills in my face.

My heart sank as Edward lifted up another book and gave it a dramatic shake. More money — along with an impressive cloud of dust — flew into the air.

"Why is she hiding money like that?" Shelley shrieked (no one could pump up the stress level in a room faster than Shelley). "I mean...does this mean...do we have to check inside *everything* we're throwing out?"

"Only the books, dear," Grandma said. She hadn't been kidding about being back in a jiffy. "That's where I hide my money — you can't trust the banks these days."

Edward was already in the groove — he'd choose a book, give it a big shake, squeal if money dropped out, then lunge for the next one. I had to admit he was handling the situation pretty well, but if he kept making that stupid noise, I was going to have to kill him.

Suddenly, a dark shadow fell across the living room. Clyde — Grandma's big, grinning, almost toothless taxi-driving neighbor — was standing in the doorway.

"Grammy tells me you've got some donations for my next car boot sale," he bellowed.

"A car boot sale is kind of like a garage sale," Edward said, peering through a cloud of dust and fluttering bills. "But in England, people don't have sales in their driveways — they rent spots at big flea markets, instead."

"Clyde just loves car boot sales — he goes once a month," Grandma said. "If you can get some things boxed up by 3 o'clock, he'll put them in tomorrow's sale."

Well, I have to tell you, I've never moved so fast in my life. Old clothes, tacky trinkets, books (minus the money, of course), useless kitchen gadgets, faded furniture, rusty tools...every piece of junk we could find went out the door as fast as we could pack it.

Everything was going beautifully. The problem was the odd look on Grandma's face. True, she was smiling, but in a sad kind of way — and there's only so long I could pretend to not notice something like that.

"What's wrong, Grandma, did you want to keep this stuff?"

Please say no...please say no...please say no...

"Well, I guess some of it, yes," she said, as she watched Shelley pull a moldy old shower curtain from under the stairs. "I know it looks like a lot of junk to you, but there are some real treasures hidden in here."

"It doesn't look like junk," I lied. "Do you want us to stop so you can go through things?"

Please say no...please say no...please say no...

"Yes, dear, thank you — but just for a minute so I can save the precious things," she said, as she poked through a beaten-up old trunk. "Like this!" Grandma smiled as she held up what looked like a battered old dollhouse — except it was filled with tiny pieces of wood that were shaped and painted to look like meat.

"Ooooh...that's a model of a traditional English butcher shop — it must be over 100 years old!" Edward wiped cobwebs out of his hair as he stepped closer for a better look. "Parents gave them to their daughters in Victorian times to teach them about different cuts of meat — girls were expected to learn about stuff like that before they got married!"

Don't be too impressed. True, Edward was a history freak, but he was also standing there with Grandma's massive bra tied around his waist like a saggy, two-pouched fanny pack, and he was using the cups — which were drooping down to his knobby knees — to hold the money he was finding on his book-shaking spree.

"Edward, you're spot on," Grandma said. "And this is

another antique — one of the few toys Victorian children were allowed to play with on Sundays." Grandma held up an old, faded Noah's Arc — complete with about 20 animals. Plus a surprisingly thick layer of dust.

"But how will we get done today if we have to pick through everything to figure out what to keep?" Shelley wailed, using her most irritating, whiney voice.

Everyone just stood there, stumped.

"Well," I sighed. "What if we make an assembly line? Grandma, if you stand in the doorway, we can pass everything through you so nothing gets out unless you give it the okay. That way you can snag the stuff you really love."

And you know what? It worked. Grandma was able to save the best of her stuff — ugly lamps, ugly pictures, ugly chairs (the fact that something's an antique doesn't mean it's pretty). And the rest of the junk went into Clyde's shed for storage until the morning's boot sale.

Soon, Grandma's place looked like a real home — a dusty, hairball-filled home, but at least you could find the important things (like countertops and floors). I took a deep breath — I still had that weird, tight feeling in my stomach, but at least now Shelley couldn't say I was being selfish. I'd done something to help Grandma.

"You're still being selfish, you know — you just helped so you could get rid of the guilt," Shelley said, as she walked past me to the kitchen (proving, once again, that her main goal in life was to suck the fun out of mine).

Luckily, Grandma chose that exact moment to take a good look around.

"Well, now, I think this place is perfect — absolutely perfect. You've done a smashing job!" Grandma unhooked Edward's freakish fanny pack and shook the money into a kitchen drawer. "Fred and I are heading down the lane for our Friday night bridge game with the girls. All I need you to do is keep Rutabaga out of harm's way until I get back in a few hours."

"Rutabaga?" Edward asked.

"Rutabaga's here!" bellowed Clyde, as he squeezed through Grandma's front door, yet again.

You're probably picturing a vegetable, right? Or a dog — a small, ugly one with a flat face. Or maybe a fluffy, snarly cat. No. Rutabaga was a parrot — one of those huge Macaws. He was almost three feet long, with shiny blue and gold feathers and (I cannot emphasize this enough) a beak that looked like it could snap off my whole thumb in one bite.

"We're baby-sitting little Rutabaga this weekend, since Clyde's taking my things to his boot sale," Grandma explained, as Clyde set the huge parrot on the back of a kitchen chair. "Rutabaga loves watching the tellee, so you four can relax and have dinner together in the lounge while I'm gone!"

Edward, Shelley and I just stood there, silent, as Grandma and her hairy old dog disappeared out the door. And when it became clear that she *wasn't* going to throw the door open and yell "surprise!" we turned around to take a closer look at...

"Oh, crud, where'd he go?" I asked, as I dropped down on my knees and looked under the table.

"A tellee is a TV." Edward loved being a know-it-all, even during a crisis. "And a lounge is a livingroo...*Ouch! Oh no! Help!*"

Edward had found Rutabaga. Actually, it would be more accurate to say that Rutabaga had found Edward. The massive bird was perched on top of Edward's head — he'd probably decided that Edward's curly, unbrushed hair would make a great nest — and he was stretching his wings in a slow, yoga kind of way.

"Get him off!" Edward shrieked. "His claws are sharp!"

It was obvious Shelley wasn't going to be any help at all — she was too busy laughing and rummaging through her purse for her camera. So I tried pushing Rutabaga off Edward's head using Grandma's umbrella. I tried prodding him off using a wooden spoon. I even tried scaring him off by flapping a newspaper in his face.

Finally, I gave up. "Just sit down on the couch," I said. "Grandma will be home in a few hours." Which, apparently, was what Edward should have done in the first place, because as soon as his scrawny little butt touched the cushions, Rutabaga hopped onto the back of the couch and strutted around, showing off like a runway model.

And, I have to admit, we had a surprisingly pleasant evening after that. We discovered that Rutabaga loves licking peanut butter off a spoon, and drinking chocolate milk out of a glass, and stealing birthday cake off people's plates.

All in all, it went really well — until Edward accidentally stepped on one of the seven dwarfs.

The cat — I'm pretty sure it was Dopey — arched his back and hissed at Edward. Big mistake. Rutabaga exploded off the couch — producing an awesome cloud of feathers and dander — flew across the room and grabbed Dopey by the tail.

"Stop him!" Shelley screamed, as she ran into the bathroom and slammed the door.

"Watch out for his claws!" Edward screamed, as he scrambled behind the couch and covered his head.

"Shut up and help me!" I screamed. I know, I know...they'd already abandoned me, but screaming made me feel a little better.

I looked around frantically for something to hit Rutabaga with. It had to be big enough to startle him into letting go of Dopey, but soft enough that it wouldn't actually *hurt* the stupid bird. The only thing I could find? Grandma's old bra, which she'd tossed over her bedroom doorknob after peeling it off Edward.

I grabbed the bra and raced back to the living room. Rutabaga was dragging Dopey backward, by his tail, across the couch. The frazzled cat was trying to hang on with his front claws while his back legs wind milled wildly in midair. I'd smacked Rutabaga with the bra — once, twice, maybe three times — when...

"What the..." It was Grandma. She was standing in the entryway, leaning against Fred in an odd, wobbly sort of way.

"What on earth?" It was Auntie Gay. She was standing behind Grandma, peering around her and scowling at me.

"I...I had to! Rutabaga attacked Dopey!" I said, trying to hide the bra behind my back (and you can imagine how successful *that* was).

I pointed to the couch...but it was empty. Rutabaga was perched on the back of a kitchen chair, calmly rocking back and forth, looking completely innocent. And Dopey? He was lying on the floor, grooming himself as if nothing had happened.

"Has everyone in this family *completely* lost their minds?" Auntie Gay asked. That was a pretty funny question, actually, coming from a woman with a big yellow bow on her shirt and a tacky flower thing sticking out of her hat.

"Oh, don't be such a fusspot." Grandma staggered over to the couch and flopped down. Fred, as if they were attached by an invisible rope, staggered along right behind her and flopped down on the floor at her feet. Suddenly, Fred burped, and Grandma burst out laughing.

"You're *drunk*!" Auntie Gay glared at her sister. "That silly bridge night of yours is nothing but an excuse to make a fool of yourself with a bunch of senile old ladies."

"They're no more senile than you are," Grandma said as she

tried, without much success, to kick off her shoes. "And maybe if *you'd* loosen up once in a while, it wouldn't have taken 64 years to find someone willing to marry you."

Well, if it was possible for someone's head to explode, that would have been the end of Auntie Gay right there. Instead, she stormed around the room, yelling, "I have *had it* with you. You have lost your mind...you're too old to take care of yourself...you're a slob...you're a drunk...your *dog* is a drunk..."

It went on and on, but you get the idea. And as her car tore out of the driveway, Edward slowly crept out of his hiding spot.

"She never even noticed how nice the house looks," he said. It was true. We'd spent all day cleaning out Grandma's house...and it hadn't done a bit of good.

Chapter 7

When Wine-Tasting Parties Go Horribly Wrong

"Auntie Gay's convinced you can't take care of yourself," Shelley said, as she tiptoed out of the bathroom. "What are you going to do?"

Grandma frowned as she tried, in vain, to fix her hair. She liked to wear it in a little gray bun, but now strands were sticking out all over the place — she looked like a teen wannabe.

"Don't get to bridges before you cross them...don't cross bridges before you get to...well, you know what I mean." And with those words of wisdom, Grandma heaved herself off the couch and headed to the bathroom. Fred staggered to his feet and followed, his mammoth butt weaving side to side like a wobbly camper trailer.

Thunk. Fred slammed, headfirst, into the wall. True, he was her faithful companion, but he also had the I.Q. of a turnip.

Fred shook his head — sending a shower of dog slobber across the room — then flopped down on the floor. When

Grandma came out of the bathroom, she stepped right over him without looking (making me suspicious that they'd done this before). Her hair — most of it, anyway — was back in its usual bun.

"Do you, uh, play bridge every Friday?" I asked.

Grandma laughed. "We *used* to play bridge, but that's an old ladies' game. We switched to winemaking last year. I didn't tell your Auntie Gay because *she* likes to think she's a teetotaler."

Edward stopped halfway up the stairs. "She likes to *think*...?" he asked.

"I've seen her get into the gin and tonic, dear," Grandma said. "It's not a pretty sight."

Grandma headed straight for the fridge and pulled out an odd assortment of wine bottles.

"Um...are you sure you should be drinking more tonight?" I asked.

"Oh, don't be silly — we're just going to have a little wine tasting session," Grandma said, laughing. "I'd like your opinion on my newest creations — and you wouldn't mind a few sips of wine, would you?"

Grandma didn't wait for an answer. She filled a big bowl with chocolate-covered peanuts ("to cleanse your palette between tastes," she explained) then uncorked one of the bottles.

The first sip was a shocker. I'd tried wine before, but nothing like this. It went right up my nose like horseradish, making my eyes water and my nose run.

"The alcohol content might be a bit high," Grandma said, as she handed me a tissue. "I'm starting to wonder if I used the wrong kind of yeast in this batch."

I glanced over at Shelley. Her eyes were wide and her nose was red — just like the time I dared her to eat Vicks VapoRub when we were kids. Even Rutabaga was making odd sniffling noises — regretting, no doubt, that he'd snuck a taste from Grandma's glass.

I finished mine as fast as I could — thankfully, Grandma had only filled my glass halfway — then watched as she uncorked the next bottle. Oddly, *this* wine looked a lot like grape soda— it even foamed right over the top when Grandma poured it. And it *tasted* a lot like grape soda, too — sweet, fruity...

"This is delicious." I tried to stifle a burp. "I didn't realize wine could taste this good."

"Well, it really isn't supposed to be like this," Grandma said, as she poured some into a bowl for Rutabaga. "I think I used too much sugar, and that's why the yeast went wild and made bubbles — I'm still learning, really."

"Grandma..." My chest felt tight. We really did need to talk about moving Grandma into a home, but I dreaded bringing it up.

"Grandma, I..."

"Oh, Monica, I know." Grandma took a swig of her grape soda wine and sighed. "Your Auntie Gay thinks it's *my* time to go into a home, and since she's the one who helped our brothers when it was their time, your mom's assuming she must be right."

Grandma glanced at the four cats that were sprawled across the kitchen counter, cleaning themselves. "And because you love things clean and tidy, you can't imagine living in, well, *this*, so you're assuming she must be right, too. So now you're trying to find some way to convince me to leave my home of almost 60 years and move into a place for people who are sitting around waiting to die."

I opened my mouth, and then clamped it shut. I mean, really, what do you say when someone crawls into your head and reads your mind? What do you say when what you've been thinking sounds really, really awful when it's said out loud?

Shelley leaned over and jabbed me with her elbow. "Nice way to wreck an evening, idiot."

Grandma looked at Shelley and then at me. Suddenly, she laughed. "It's impossible to wreck an evening as long as you have homemade wine!" she said, as she popped the cork out of another bottle.

"URP!" Rutabaga said, shaking his head. Turned out Grandma's wine could even make a parrot burp.

I'll be honest, the next bottle of wine was sickening. Grandma called it a "dry white," but I thought it tasted more like cough syrup (although I drank the glass to be polite, of course). Luckily, Grandma had a second bottle of grape soda wine in the fridge, so I was able to get rid of the nasty cough syrup aftertaste.

"This one's rully grood Glamma," I said. "I mean...it's glood, Gamma..." Rats. What was wrong with my tongue?

Grandma's eyebrows slid up her face and she tried not to laugh. Shelley wasn't even trying to hold it in — she was giggling like a fool.

"Nice going, Monica," Shelley said, as she tossed a chocolate-covered peanut into her mouth. Sadly — for her, at least — it bounced off her cheek and rolled across the floor into the living room.

"Monica, go get the door, please," Grandma said.

The door? I hadn't heard a knock, but if Grandma wanted me to get the door, I'd get the door.

I couldn't get the door.

It was the weirdest thing. I could stand up. But when I tried to walk, well, my legs just didn't have a clue. To move one foot — which is pretty much a necessity if you're trying to get to a door — I had to lift that knee up, then kind of throw the whole leg forward and hope it landed a reasonable distance in front of my body. Which sometimes it didn't. I looked like a spastic robot in one of those old late-night movies. I finally made it to the door, but no matter how hard I tried to turn the knob, nothing happened.

I'd pretty much given up when, quite suddenly, the door flew open. And since my hand was still attached to the knob, I staggered outside and into the arms of the most gorgeous guy I'd ever seen in my life. He was tall and had broad shoulders, dark, thick hair, huge brown eyes and ridiculously long lashes. Plus he smelled wonderful — as if he'd just climbed out of a hot, soapy shower and then decided to find me and sweep me off my feet. He was absolute perfection.

I looked up so that I could gaze longingly into his eyes, but my head — which was wobbling around like a bowling ball on a stick — snapped too far back. After gazing longingly at the top of his head for a few seconds, I tried (again) to find his eyes, but my bowling ball rolled too far forward and I ended up gazing longingly at his chest.

"Tank oo fur...catching me," I said to his chest. Rats. Still couldn't talk right.

"Clyde, great to see you!" Grandma called, as she waved him in.

Clyde? Old, grinning, toothless taxi-driving Clyde? Apparently, I was hallucinating. I stepped back to get a better look, tripped over the doorframe and landed on my butt.

I didn't need to turn around to know that the wheezing sound coming from the kitchen was Shelley — she was laughing so hard she'd hit that point where all you can really hope is that you won't snort like a pig. Grandma, I'm relieved to say, was ignoring her.

"Monica, Shelley, you've met Clyde," she said. "Well, this is his son, Clyde Junior. He's 16." I barely heard her, of course, because the most gorgeous guy I'd ever seen in my entire life was pulling me to my feet. He gazed into my eyes for at least two seconds (trust me, it was Heaven) before looking around the room.

There was a lot to look at. Edward — who'd been hiding upstairs during our wine tasting party — had stuck his head through the hole in the ceiling and was making stupid faces at us. Shelley and Grandma were slumped over the table, surrounded by empty bottles and wine glasses. And Rutabaga...

"Oh, Rutabaga, not again!" Clyde Junior said. Rutabaga was walking across the table toward us. Oddly, he was leaning over sideways — like he was using a cane that was too short. And when he got to the table's edge, instead of spreading his wings and flying gracefully (as parrots supposedly do), he simply continued walking...straight off the table and beak-first onto the floor.

Thonk. A cloud of feathers floated up into the air.

"I see you folks have been tasting Grammy's homemade wine," Clyde said, smiling. "I just came to tell you that I picked up my suit for your Aunt's wedding — and that I'll be coming on my own."

"You're coming to the wedding? Without a date?" Shelley asked.

Suddenly, Shelley lunged out of her chair, knocking it onto the floor (she'd had a lot of the grape soda wine, and it was really starting to show). She sauntered across the room toward Clyde, wiggling her massive boobs as she walked. She looked like an idiot. She looked like a tramp. Yes, I was jealous.

Since I had nothing to wiggle, I decided to sit down and look intelligent. I plunked my elbow on the table and rested my chin on my hand. Sadly, I wasn't as close to the table as I'd thought. My elbow skidded right off the edge and my head jerked down — hard. I didn't smack my face on the table, but I came dangerously close.

Luckily, Clyde hadn't noticed. He hadn't noticed anything since Shelley had started batting her eyes and flicking her hair around.

"So, where do you work?" she asked, in a low, breathless voice. Barf.

"Well, I'm still in school, but I work at the Titty Ho Garage on weekends," he said. Shelley looked confused, but then wiggled her boobs at him, again.

"What do you do there?" she asked.

I have no idea what he said — although "fix cars" would probably sum it up nicely — because of Rutabaga. Ever watch a parrot climb a tree? Well, Rutabaga climbed up the table leg like it was a tree — biting the wood, pulling himself up, biting the wood, pulling himself up...one boozy step at a time. And when he finally got to the top, he stood up, tall and proud, flapped his wings really hard...and fell backward onto the floor, again.

Rutabaga was halfway through his second climb up the table leg when Clyde made his escape. "Must go!" He grinned (at me!) as he backed out the door. "I'll see you at the wedding."

Shelley stood gazing out the window as Clyde disappeared down the road.

"You can put your boobs away, now, he's gone," I said.

"Bite me," Shelley muttered, as she staggered over to the couch. Apparently, she wasn't feeling much better than I was.

"We need to do something," I said. "We need to prove that Grandma's not nuts. You know, maybe she could stay here just fine if she had a live-in housekeeper. Maybe then Mom would be happy and would stop worrying." And maybe, just maybe, I could still get my science trip.

"I am not nuts," Grandma said, peering through the empty wine bottles. "And I do not need a live-in housekeeper."

"Ugh," Shelley said.

"We need to prove that Auntie Gay's the one who's nuts," I said.

"She *is* nuts," the wine bottles said.

"Ugh," Shelley added.

"We need..." I was stumped. I couldn't stand the guilt — but couldn't stand the thought of losing my one glorious trip-of-a-lifetime, either. There had to be some way to fix this mess.

"You know...if we can catch Auntie Gay doing something really weird, then Mom won't believe her when she claims there's something wrong with *Grandma*," I said. "If we spy on Auntie Gay, maybe we can catch her doing something that'll make *her* look senile!"

Edward stuck his arm through the hole in the ceiling and waved wildly. "Oh, Monica, please let me help! I was born to spy!"

It was true, actually. If there was one thing Edward was great at, it was skulking around spying on people when they thought they were alone. It was a little creepy, actually.

"Ugh." Shelley was curled up in a ball, holding her stomach. "Forget it. I am *not* coming."

She came, of course — it gave her an excuse to whine.

"I feel like crud," she said, as we walked down the road toward Auntie Gay's house.

"I'm going to throw up," she said, as we tiptoed across Auntie Gay's front yard.

"I hate you," she said, as we climbed Auntie Gay's huge tree.

We were making decent progress, despite Shelley's whining. And I'm pretty sure we would have discovered something really good — something that would have made Auntie Gay look like a complete nut — if only someone hadn't seen us.

"Oi! What are you doing up there?" I looked down to see where the booming voice was coming from. It was coming from the policeman who was standing directly below Shelley's branch, shining his light up at us.

My stomach lurched as Edward opened his mouth. "We're spying on our great-aunt," he yelled. "We want to make her look nutty so our grandma won't be sent to an old folks' home. Monica thinks someone should come babysit her, but that's because Monica's a perfectionist. Shelley's been completely useless, but that's because she's drunk."

"I am compete...complete...completely sober," Shelley said, as she stared down at the man who was, I was convinced, about to throw us in jail for life.

You know, I've always believed that there is no problem so great that it can't, somehow, be made infinitely worse. Which was why I wasn't the slightest bit surprised that Shelley chose that exact moment to throw up.

Chapter 8

Hangovers…They're Not For Sissies

Silence. That was the worst part of the whole thing. If he'd yelled at us, dragged us out of the tree — hey, even *shot* at us — it would have been easier to take. But he didn't. Instead, he calmly took three steps back and just stood there, waiting.

So we climbed down gracefully (tried to, anyway). Then listened in silence as he lectured us about the perils of heavy drinking and the importance of knowing our limits, while streams of purple vomit trickled down his uniform.

I'd never felt so guilty in my entire life — and *I* wasn't even the one who'd thrown up on him. One thing was certain: the night could not get any worse.

"What the *hell?*" It was Auntie Gay. She was standing on her front porch wearing a bright orange fluffy robe and slippers. Her hair was wrapped around huge green curlers, and there was some sort of thick white cream all over her face. She looked like a Pez dispenser. A very angry Pez dispenser.

"Please put us in jail," Edward whispered. But the policeman didn't answer — he was staring, speechless, at Auntie

Gay.

"This is your grandmother's fault!" Auntie Gay screamed (at all four of us — which really wasn't fair, if you think about it). "That woman cannot take care of herself, or anyone else, for that matter. She's a hazard!"

Auntie Gay slammed her front door so hard that the windows rattled, then stormed down the lane toward Grandma's house — still in her slippers, bathrobe and curlers. "Hurry up," she yelled over her shoulder. "I have had enough of this nonsense!"

"Please put us in jail," Edward whispered, again, as he watched Auntie Gay stomp down the road.

"No need," the policeman said, with a tight little smile. "Looks like you're going to be punished enough as it is."

And with that, he left.

Of course, what Grandma *should* have done when we got to her house was look embarrassed, apologize for letting two drunk teenagers and a hyperactive boy out of her sight and promise to never, ever, let it happen again.

But we're talking about Grandma, here. So the first thing she did was burst out laughing (couldn't blame her, really — Auntie Gay looked ridiculous). And the second thing she did was, well, not very helpful, either.

"Oh, for Heaven's sake, Gay, they're just kids. Kids make mistakes." Grandma flopped down in her favorite chair, as Edward raced upstairs to hide (he's not stupid, that's for sure).

"Kids? *Kids*? They're old enough to get drunk, which means they're old enough to take care of themselv...no, I mean, *you* were supposed to be taking care of th...I mean...aaarrrggghh! You are so frustrating!"

Auntie Gay must have needed a break from her tirade, because she stopped yelling and stood there, glaring — at the heap of dirty dishes in the sink, the cats sauntering across the counter, the newspapers scattered across the coffee table...

Then she watched, in horror, as Rutabaga chose that exact moment — truly the worst timing imaginable — to poop on the kitchen table.

"That's it," Auntie Gay said, shaking her head. "I've already called the care home and they've agreed to take you Tuesday. We're packing your belongings right after the wedding."

"But, Auntie Gay, couldn't we just get Grandma a live-in housekeeper?" My heart was pounding so loudly I could hear it in my ears. I had never argued with an angry Pez dispenser before — and I have to tell you, it was a little scary.

Auntie Gay turned and stared coldly at me. "And what would *that* accomplish?"

"Well, then maybe she would be just fine, and everyone would be happy without her leaving her home."

Auntie Gay narrowed her eyes. "*Everyone* would be happy? What are you trying to pull? Do you know how much a live-in housekeeper costs?"

"I'm...I'm just trying to find some sort of compromise. Maybe if we got Grandma's place...nicer, and got someone who could keep it that way, she could stay here." I moved my elbows away from my sides — my armpits were sweating like mad.

Auntie Gay shook her head in disgust. "You'd have to burn this place down to make it look nice — *you*, of all people, know that this is a disastrous mess." And with that, Auntie Gay stormed out the front door — slamming it hard, in true diva fashion — and the house fell silent.

"This is Friday...Auntie Gay's wedding is on Monday," Edward said. "In three days we'll be packing up Grandma's things."

"You know, Monica, you're making it worse," Shelley said.

I'd kind of forgotten about Shelley. She'd propped herself up against the fridge when we'd gotten home and, like a fridge magnet holding up too many papers, she'd been slowly, steadily, sliding down the door. A few more inches and she'd be sitting on the floor.

"Mom's coming as soon as she can," I said. "We just need to prove to *her* that we can fix this place up and get Grandma help."

"You're completely missing the point," said the fridge magnet. "Mom won't agree to a live-in housekeeper — we can't afford it — and you're still hung up on making Grandma into a clean freak like you."

"I…I'm trying to think. Shut up and let me think." I rocked from one foot to the other as I tried to clear my head.

"Cripes, I'm sick of this." It was the fridge magnet, again. "You act so prissy and noble, but you're in it for that stupid science trip, and you know it."

I peeked at Grandma out of the corner of my eye. "Stop it, Shelley. You know that's not true."

"Sure it is. And now you're feeling guilty, so you're looking for some stupid compromise so you can make Mom happy and get your trip. You don't care that Grandma doesn't want *any* of this."

"Shelley, please…" Would she ever shut up? I swallowed hard, fighting back tears.

Truth is, I *did* want that trip — more than I'd wanted anything in my life. If Grandma was in a senior's home — or at least had a housekeeper — it meant she'd be taken care of, and I'd have the best August of my life. I wasn't being completely selfish. But I wasn't proud of myself, either.

"Oh, Monica, it's okay — I do remember a bit about what it's like to be a teenager." Grandma sighed sadly. "But this has been my home for almost 60 years. I can't imagine leaving."

"Grandma, please...please consider getting a housekeeper. You do need help — and maybe that would be enough to make Mom happy and to stop Auntie Gay."

Shelley just glared at me.

"Why don't you...why don't you take us on a tour of London?" I asked. "We could look at the sites, take pictures. If you organize a big trip, that'll prove to Mom that you can take care of yourself just fine, don't you think?"

Grandma looked at me and smiled (but a bit sadly).

"I suppose that might work. Let's leave first thing in the morning." The fridge magnet just groaned.

I went to bed with thoughts of London rolling through my head. It was going to be an amazing day.

Or not.

Ever heard someone say they felt like "death warmed over?" When I woke up Saturday morning, I found out exactly what that phrase meant. My head felt thick and clammy, like it was stuck inside a giant watermelon. And the giant watermelon was filled with tiny little gnomes who were sticking tiny little forks into my eyeballs. My stomach lurched around wildly, full of stuff it had absolutely no intention of digesting. My legs, my arms...they were so heavy, I could barely move them.

I'm not exaggerating, either. *You* try combining jet lag with too much wine, then climb a tree, get almost arrested and then spend the night sleeping with a massive, squirming dog that won't get off your bed and see how *you* feel. You'll feel like death warmed over, that's how you'll feel.

Of course, as I've mentioned before, I truly believe there's no situation so terrible that it can't, somehow, be made infinitely worse. So I stood up.

Suddenly, Grandma's striped wallpaper wasn't covered with stripes, anymore. It was covered with wavy lines that were, well, *waving* — I really don't know how else to describe it. And the gnomes started poking at my eyeballs with mega-sized forks.

I tried to sit down, but missed the edge of the bed. Which — to make a long story short — was why I ended up crawling on my hands and knees to the stairs, then crawling backward down the stairs into the living room. I looked stupid, I know, but it was a lot less nauseating than fighting the wavy wallpaper. Thankfully, it was still early, so no one would be awake to see me.

"Good morning, Monica!" Edward bellowed, as he shook open the newspaper and spread it across the table (don't be too impressed — he only reads the cartoons).

"Edward, please don't yell," I said, as I pressed my palms into my eyeballs, trying to squish the gnomes. "And please don't flap the paper so loudly."

"That's exactly what Shelley said," Edward bellowed — he really only had one volume. "Although *she* didn't say please."

Shelley. It took me a minute to focus but, sure enough, there she was — slumped over the kitchen table, her hair hanging over her face.

"I'll get you a coffee." Edward leapt out of his seat. "I made it myself."

"The caffeine will help you," Shelley muttered. "I'm feeling a lot better now."

I sat down slowly as Edward set a big mug in front of me. One sip and my eyes shot open — wide open. Suddenly, I was struggling to swallow what I'd just put in my mouth, while my stomach fought valiantly to shove it right back up, again.

"What *is* this?" I asked, as I wiped the tears from my eyes.

"Coffee," he said, looking irritated — clearly, he'd gotten the same kind of reaction from Shelley. "I mixed four tablespoons of instant coffee powder with four tablespoons of powdered milk, then filled the cup with hot tap water and stirred in some sugar. It's basically the same as regular coffee, but I didn't have to boil water, so it's more energy efficient."

Shelley lifted her head just long enough to give me a snotty look. "I said it would help. I didn't say it tasted good."

Cripes. Even hungover, she was still a witch.

Suddenly, the bathroom door flew open and Grandma stomped out in an enormous, fluffy housecoat. "Time to go! I've got the perfect outfits for us!" Grandma scurried across the room and pulled a big bag out from under the stairs.

She turned the bag upside down and out fell...

"Stripes?" Edward asked.

"Stripes!" Grandma said, grinning. She lifted up a short, wide pair of pants absolutely covered with bright stripes — every color of the rainbow, plus a few colors that no discriminating rainbow would even consider displaying. "These are mine, of course."

Then she lifted up a short, ridiculously narrow pair. "And these are for you, Edward."

Two longer pairs followed. "One pair for you, and one pair for you," Grandma said, smiling at Shelley and me. "And look! Matching shirts!"

The good news? The shirts weren't striped. The bad news? They were the most hideous shade of green I'd ever seen. Fluorescent frog puke — that's what Crayola would have called it (not that Crayola would even consider making a color that nauseating).

"I had matching outfits made," Grandma said, stating what was already painfully obvious. "I thought we could have fun with them — perhaps drive your Auntie Gay batty by wearing them to the wedding rehearsal. But they'll be perfect for today's adventure. Plus they're silly and fun — and there's nothing wrong with being silly and fun, is there, Edward?"

"Nothing at all," said Edward, who'd already pulled on the pants and was wrestling into the hideous shirt.

Grandma tossed a pair of striped pants and a frog puke shirt over her arm and stomped off toward her bedroom. Like she was going to *wear* them. Like she figured *we* were going to wear them!

"Get dressed, girls — these outfits will make it easier for us to find each other in crowds," Grandma called from her room. "We need to get rolling — there's lots to do in London, but first we have to drive to Bedford and find parking, then catch a train to the Thameslink Station, then take the underground to Piccadilly..."

Or something like that. I'm not sure exactly what she said, because I was a little distracted by the pants in my hands.

"Come on, genius," Shelley said, as she staggered to the bathroom. "You wanted to do this stupid trip — now you can *look* stupid while you do it."

The next few minutes were a blur, but somehow Shelley and I got dressed, brushed our teeth and got into the car. The possible highlights of the morning? Neither of us barfed — and I didn't go blind looking at all of our striped pants during the long, quiet drive.

"Hmmmm..." Grandma said, as she pulled into the Bedford train station.

"What does hmmmm mean?" Edward asked, as he smoothed down his pants for probably the millionth time.

"Hmmmm means...well, I'm just a little surprised."

Grandma slowly cruised through the parking lot, looking for a free space. "I don't understand why it's so busy, today. I hope you won't mind walking a bit."

I looked at myself in the rear view mirror and tried to focus on the pasty-faced, puffy-eyed stranger staring back at me. "Sure, Grandma, whatever you need us to do."

"Are you nuts?" Shelley hissed. "I feel like crap — and we look like morons. We can't *walk* anywhere."

"Three days, Shelley," I hissed right back. "We have three days to prove Grandma can get by with just a housekeeper."

"You're an idiot," Shelley muttered, as she slowly — very slowly — climbed out of the car. Apparently, the fork-carrying gnomes were poking at *her* eyeballs, too. Good.

"I cannot *wait* to see the Tower of London," Edward said, as we were swept along with the crowd into the jam-packed train. "And Westminster Abbey, and Buckingham Palace and…"

"Where are we going to start?" I asked Grandma.

"Oh, Heavens, I have no idea." Grandma handed Edward the camera and started searching for a seat.

"But you have a plan, right? You know where we should go?"

"No idea at all," Grandma said, laughing. "I never go into the city — this will be my first trip in 31 years."

Shelley and I looked at each other — nauseous, tired, and now a little panicked.

"Hey, look, there's a subway stop in a place called Cockfosters!" Edward yelled, as he snapped photos of the train's huge wall-mounted map.

Click…click…click…

Sometimes, the best way to deal with Edward is to ignore him. This was one of those times.

"But Grandma! If you don't know anything about London, how can you take us on a tour that'll impress Mom?" I asked.

Click…click…click…

Edward had been given a simple task — take photos of our trip to make Grandma look good — and, as usual, he'd gone completely obsessive-compulsive about it.

"No one said *I* had to be the official tour guide," Grandma said, as she smiled at Edward.

"Oh, Grandma, please don't let *him* show us around London," Shelley said.

"It'll be brilliant," Grandma replied. "He's very intelligent, he's a huge fan of British history, and he knows all the important sites. Plus he's aces at reading maps."

All true, but I didn't need to be happy — or even gracious — about it. Just thinking about following that little know-it-all snot around London made me sick. Just being with him on the train was making me irritable. But, truth was, I didn't have a clue how to get to Westminster Abbey, let alone why it was such a big deal. History really wasn't my thing.

"Ooooh, look at this!" squealed our future Tour Guide From Hell. "There's a place near here called Cockayne! We should go there, Grandma!"

Click...click...click...

"Edward, stop it!" I yelled (okay, I *wanted* to yell, but I was stuck doing that hissing thing, again, since we were surrounded by strangers).

And you know what made it worse? Thanks to our stupid matching outfits, a lot of those strangers were taking pictures of *us*.

"Um, Monica..." Shelley was poking me in the ribs. I hate it when she does that, so I ignored her.

"You need to pick educational places to visit — like it's a school trip or something," I said to Edward. "Nothing weird or...or any place with *cock* in the name."

"Monica..." Cripes, Shelley was a pain.

"It has to look like Grandma's a good role model," I said.

"Monica!" Shelley jabbed me in the ribs. Hard. "I found out why the train's so crowded." We screeched to a stop in the Thameslink Station. "It's Gay Pride day — they're expecting a million extra people in London, and a lot of them are going to look like...*that*."

She was pointing at a group of men — at least I think they were men — walking past the train. Men wearing more makeup than even the sluttiest girls at school, plus huge sparkly earrings, high heels, and dresses with slits that showed off their underwear.

My stomach churned. "It'll be okay," I whispered to Shelley. "As long as Mom doesn't find out about this, we'll be fine."

Click...

Sadly, I'd forgotten about our scrawny tour guide and his trusty camera.

Chapter 9

A Really Stinky Day

"Hey, look at this!" Edward yelled. He'd grabbed a newspaper that someone had left on the train. And as we were being swept out onto the platform with all the other passengers — holding onto our short, striped Granny so we wouldn't lose her in the crowd — he started yelling out the headlines: *Gay Pride Day! National Cricket Championship Finals! Concert to Benefit African AIDS Orphans!*

"They're saying an extra three million people could be in London today," Edward yelled. "Can you imagine? It's going to be bedlam!"

Bedlam hardly described it. Clots of half-dressed men wearing women's dresses and high heels — plus a year's supply of shockingly bright makeup — were mincing around the station.

"They look ridiculous," Shelley muttered, as she checked her lipstick in a store window. "Don't they realize green eye shadow is out?"

Apparently not. They also didn't seem to realize that green eye shadow was supposed to be applied with a makeup brush, not a paint roller...and that you were supposed to wear *pants* over your underwear. I'm not kidding — there were men walking around wearing women's undies, big curly blonde wigs, paint-rollered makeup...and nothing else. *Nothing else!*

"Close your mouth, dear," Grandma said. "Some of these blokes are being pretty daft about it, but I'm quite sure you've seen men dressed in drag before."

I was quite sure that I hadn't. And I was equally sure that I had never — not once in my entire life — been caught in a doorway with my face squished into a man's white lacy bra and stubbly, shaved chest.

Now, sadly, I can say that I have.

I wish I could tell you that we had an amazing, eye-opening adventure that day. But just getting off the train and struggling along the platform to the stairs was so traumatic that, well, basically we chickened out.

"Anyone interested in tea?" Grandma asked brightly.

"Only if it's in Bedford," I said, while Edward — who was clinging to me like a drowning puppy — nodded wildly. Thameslink station was not a good place for a short, skinny, squishable little troll.

So here's how our trip to London went: We got off the train, got squished, crossed over to the other side of the building and got *onto* a train heading the opposite direction. Yep, we spent exactly seven minutes and 13 seconds in London — and we were in a grimy, smelly train station the whole time. I've heard it's a beautiful city.

"No worries," Grandma said, as she settled into her seat. "There are lots of fun things to do back in Bedford."

Shelley just sighed loudly as she stared out the window. She was trying to make a point, of course. Shelley had been planning on sweeping through the city like some glamor queen — you should have *seen* all the mascara she'd gobbed on in the car — and now she was going to spend the day hungover in the not-so-glamorous town of Bedford (population 79,190).

"Well, at least we can sit down, now," Edward said, as he bounced from seat to seat, trying to find the one with the best view of London (a city we were probably never going to visit in our entire lives).

When we got to the train station in Bedford, I was sweaty, headachy and tired. So you can imagine how relieved I was to see Grandma's car in the parking lot. And you can imagine how relieved I was when we climbed in and put on our seat belts. And you can imagine how relieved I was when Grandma stuck the key in the ignition and...

Rrrr...rrrr...rrrr...

"Dammit to hell," Grandma said. "The bloody battery's dead."

So we got out of the car. Slowly. Reluctantly. Hoping, by some miracle, that the stupid thing would suddenly start. Although the fact that Grandma was storming back to the train station — with the keys in her hand — meant our chances were getting slimmer by the minute.

Grandma was already talking on a pay phone when we found her. And it didn't take long to figure out who she was talking to, either.

"Because they *wanted* to see London, and normally that wouldn't have been a problem, you fussy old cow!" she said, scowling.

And with her voice rising so loud that even Edward glanced around to see who was watching..."No, I did *not* bring my vitamins. Just feed the damned dog!"

And with that, she hung up.

"Honestly, she is the most irritating woman I have ever

known," Grandma mumbled, as she dialed another number. "I can't believe we're related."

"Who are you calling now?" Edward asked.

"Clyde Senior. We need to get that bloody car fixed."

As Grandma chatted with Clyde, I glanced around the station. Dozens of people were watching the news on wall-mounted TVs, yakking on their cell phones, talking to their families. They were all waiting to cram onto the next train to London. And more people were flooding in through the big doors every minute. It was bedlam.

Thankfully, Clyde would be coming to help us soon. So we could get back to Grandma's house. So I could sleep. And sleep and sleep and sleep. I couldn't remember the last time I'd felt so tired. Even my legs felt heavy.

I stepped closer to Grandma (yes, I was eavesdropping, if you must know).

"Don't hurry, dear. There's lots we can do here," she said. "After tea will be just fine."

Grandma hung up the phone and turned, smiling. "Clyde will be here right after his tea."

"So we'd better get back to the car and wait for him? We can go home soon?" I couldn't hide my relief.

Grandma shook her head and grinned. "No, silly, tea means his evening meal. We've got all day to travel around Bedford."

I couldn't hide my horror. I was filthy and hungry, my head throbbed and I needed a nap. No, not a nap. Something more than that. A 12-hour coma, perhaps.

"What's wrong?" she asked.

What do you say when *everything's* wrong? When you feel like crap — and look worse? When you're wearing the ugliest outfit you've ever seen? When you've got the worst case of jet lag imaginable, plus a wicked hangover?

"I'm…hungry, I guess."

Grandma brightened right up. "No problem," she said. "We'll get curry!"

And with that, she stomped down the street. She didn't even check behind her — just assumed we'd follow her. Which, of course, we did.

"We're eating *curry*?" Shelley scrunched up her nose as if Grandma had offered us maggot stew. "*Curry*?"

"Curry's a big thing in England," Edward said, as we raced to keep up with Grandma. "They have loads of different curries to choose from — East Indian cuisine is hugely popular, here."

So, with stripes and frog puke flapping in the breeze, we followed Grandma around the corner and straight into the first restaurant we found. It was crammed full of people — the lunch crowd — and, of course, they all briefly fell silent when we stomped through the door in our matching outfits. We looked weird. They were judging us and would be whispering about us while they finished their lunches. Some of them would probably even take pictures of us when we weren't looking.

Frankly, I didn't give a shit.

"This place smells amazing," I said, as I took a huge sniff.

"That's the curry." Edward was sniffing, too. "It's sweet and spicy and very tasty — at least that's what I've read."

"Ew," Shelley said. "Seriously. Ew." Shelley's just like that.

"You," Grandma said, grinning at Edward. "Are about to *experience* life, instead of just reading about it." She turned to the waitress. "We'd like your six most popular curries, please. And don't tell us what they are – we want to be surprised!"

So we sampled one amazing curry dish after another. Curries, I discovered, ranged from mild, sweet vegetable dishes to beef and chicken meals so spicy they could set your sinuses on fire. It was fabulous, and I think I ate more than Grandma, Shelley and Edward combined.

"Oh, wow…my nose…this one's really…oh…" Edward reached for his soda and blinked back tears.

"Wonderful, isn't it?" Grandma asked, as she dabbed beads of sweat off her forehead. Shelley just frowned as she picked at the food on her plate. She'd decided she was going to hate it, so she hated it. Shelley really was just like that.

"So," Grandma said, when her plate was clean. "A quick trip to the loo and we'll figure out what to do for the day."

Edward's head shot up. "Oh! Woburn Abbey! Woburn Abbey, please!"

Then, putting on his snotty, know-it-all look, he turned to Shelley and me. "Woburn is the home of the Duke and Duchess of Bedford. Monks started building it in 1145, and now it's enormous. You simply *cannot* visit England without touring at least one castle like Woburn. And it's probably only about 16 miles from here!"

Apparently, none of us had the energy to argue with him because, 20 minutes later, we were lounging around in the back of another one of England's ridiculously huge cabs, bouncing down the back roads to the castle.

Grandma — who'd eaten a fair bit of curry — quickly drifted off to sleep.

"So, how's your half-baked plan to pitch Grandma into a home going?" Shelley whispered. "Looking forward to your science trip, you selfish little freak?"

"Don't be an ass," I hissed. "You see how she's living — you know she needs help." I ignored Shelley's dramatic eye roll. "If we can convince her to get some live-in help, maybe that'll be enough to make Mom and Auntie Gay happy."

"And *you* happy. Don't forget that — because that's *so* important to everyone else," Shelley muttered.

I ignored her snotty comment — I'd had a lot of practice.

"We need to figure out how to fix this so Grandma ends up looking good."

I glared at Shelley. She was going to make another pissy comment, I just knew it. If she said one stupid word, I was going to punch her right in the head.

"We lie," Edward said, matter-of-factly, as he wiped his nose (he'd tried the hottest curry just before we left the restaurant, and it had done some pretty serious sinus damage). "We say the trip was fabulous, and Grandma was a great tour guide."

"Fine," Shelley said

"Well...I...alright," I said. His plan sounded kind of lame, but I couldn't come up with anything better. "So we tell them Grandma treated us to an amazing curry lunch and an amazing trip to Woburn Abbey. We tell them it was fun. It *will* be fun," I said.

Silly me.

The thing I hadn't realized about curry, you see, is that it's a spice you should not eat in large quantities. At least not the first time you try it.

You need to build up your digestive stamina for curry. You need to build up your intestinal endurance. You need to build up *something* before trying six huge servings of curry.

Instead, I'd shown a shocking lack of respect for my digestive tract by eating everything Grandma had offered — and eating a lot of it, too. So my digestive tract decided to show a shocking lack of respect for me. I started feeling...odd. Bloated, crampy, a little queasy. Just...odd.

My stomach gurgled loudly.

"Monica!" Edward squealed. "Isn't this going to be fabulous?"

"Well, I don't know if I'd say fabulous..."

Shelley peeled her lips back into that fake half-smile that she does so well. "Sure it will be, because we get to visit this wonderful place in our cute little matching outfits."

Grandma stretched and yawned. "We'll have a fabulous time," she said, nodding.

I wasn't really paying attention to them. I was completely preoccupied with all the gruesome sounds coming from my belly.

And that's when it happened. I sneezed.

And farted.

How can I possibly describe that fart? It was like a sudden, explosive thunderclap, followed by the sound an angry duck would make if someone stepped on it. And the smell...

"What crawled up your butt and died?" Shelley asked, as she frantically rolled down her window.

"Monica's new to the curry scene!" Edward yelled to the taxi driver, who burst out laughing as he (and I cringe to even mention this) quickly rolled down *his* window.

You'd think an event like that would easily qualify as The Most Horrendous Experience Of My Entire Life. Sadly, The Most Horrendous Experience Of My Entire Life wasn't due to occur for another 28 hours — but I'm not going to dwell on that right now.

"Don't worry, dear, it takes a while to get used to curry," Grandma said, no doubt thinking she was making me feel better. Which she wasn't.

My stomach gurgled again. My intestines were now producing enough gas to have a measurable impact on the earth's ecosystem.

By the time we got to Woburn Abbey, my belly was so swollen I looked pregnant. As we walked up to the main entrance, I purposefully lagged behind and tried to let out as many silent farts as I could. It didn't make any difference. My intestines were producing curry fumes as quickly as I could sneak them out. I was a human fart factory, and my only wish was to stay outdoors as long as possible.

"It's getting hot — let's head inside!" Grandma said, proving once again that if you're basically a good, hardworking person, and you wish for something really, really hard, it doesn't make a damned bit of difference.

Chapter 10

The Saturday That Refused
To End

"Oooooh, look at this!" Edward squealed. "They're starting a tour!" Without another word, he leapt over a flowerbed and latched himself onto a cluster of old, old, *old* East Indian women. There must have been 30 of them, and they were all short, hunched over and wizened-up. They looked like mummified midgets. And they were wearing traditional saris — those brightly colored dresses made of huge, silky pieces of fabric. It was like looking through a colorful kaleidoscope. It was like...hey...

Edward smiled and nodded when he saw my eyebrows shoot up. "No one will even notice what we're wearing if we stay with this group," he whispered, as soon as I got within earshot. "They're as colorful as we are!"

It was true. Standing alone, Edward looked like an idiot in his striped pants and vomitous green shirt. But standing with that group of wizened old ladies in their amazing saris, he almost disappeared. It was as if Edward was a chameleon — and he'd discovered the one type of scenery that frog puke could disappear into. It was brilliant!

Following Edward's lead, we clung like leeches to the sari'd seniors as they shuffled through Woburn. And it was a great tour. It really was. We saw the breakfast room, the state dining room, and the regular dining room (did the British ever stop eating?). We saw bedrooms with gaudy, gold-covered ceilings, a vault filled with silver and gold dishes, a crypt full of porcelain, hundreds of old portraits, thousands of antiques and, quite possibly, some of the ugliest wallpaper ever created (proving, I suppose, that money and good taste don't always go together). It didn't take long to realize Edward was right — you simply *cannot* visit England without touring at least one castle.

And you know what else I realized? East Indian women eat East Indian food. Which means curry. Which means not one of them was looking at me funny with a scrunched up nose (like Shelley was). I was walking through the biggest, oldest, most amazing house I'd ever seen — one that I could never hope to actually live in — yet, for the first time in days, I felt at home.

"I could live here," I said, as we walked down the wide, carpeted hall.

"You could, but you can't," Shelley said, as she stared up at the fancy chandelier.

"What do you mean?"

"*You* think that if you work hard enough, you can achieve anything — and fix anything. But sometimes you can't. Some things are just out of your control."

"Oh, I don't know about that..."

"It's true," Shelley said, frowning. "The people who lived here were born here — born into this stinking rich family. You weren't. So they're in, and you're out. Some things are just out of your control."

It was official. Shelley could even suck the fun out of daydreaming about living in a castle.

"So, what's a ha-ha?" I asked Edward, hoping to change the subject. I already knew it was a ditch thing used to keep wildlife out of rich people's gardens, but figured I'd give him the thrill of being a know-it-all. "Edward?"

I spun around full circle, looking for our pint-sized chameleon. I saw saris — lots and lots of saris — but no Edward.

"Monica, where is he?" Shelley whispered.

"Who?" Grandma asked, although the way her eyes were nervously darting around the room suggested she had a pretty good idea who we were looking for.

"Don't panic," I whispered. "If we find him before he does anything stupid, it'll be okay."

Ever tried searching for someone without looking like you're searching for someone? It isn't easy. I looked under the lumpy old bed by pretending I'd dropped something. I snuck a peak inside the fireplace by straightening my socks. I even managed a quick look inside a big dresser thing while the East Indian ladies were looking out a window and yakking in some foreign language. The window...

"Oh, no." Shelley was staring over their heads at the massive cedar tree outside (planted in 1754, Edward had informed us). "Oh, no."

I followed her gaze. It was Edward, of course, perched on a thick branch way up off the ground — and looking surprisingly parrot-like, thanks to his outfit. He was dropping nuts onto the heads of innocent passersby. The King of Stupid Pranks had struck again.

"His clothes match ours — they'll know he's with us," Shelley whispered. "Somebody's going to call the police!"

This stunk. If Edward fell out of that tree, he'd crack his head open for sure. He'd whine for days and Mom would be ticked off that I hadn't taken better care of him. And it would pretty much prove, as far as Auntie Gay was concerned, that Grandma was completely incompetent. I mean, really, who breaks their grandson the first time they take him out in public?

Shelley turned and glared at me. "If he gets wrecked, they'll toss Grandma in a home, for sure," Shelley said, doing some weird sort of mind-reading thing. "If that happens, I'll blame you forever, and you will never hear the end of this. Never."

It was true. Shelley was very good — freakishly good — at holding grudges. It was another one of her special skills that made me want (no, *need*) to get away from her this August.

"I'm trying to make a stupid compromise, you know," I said. "No senior's home — just live-in help — but if we don't get that idiot out of that tree, nothing we do will even matter."

Powered by another curry fart, I raced out the door and across the huge lawn to the tree. Then, using the kindest, gentlest, most patient voice I could muster, I called up to Edward, "You're wrecking *everything*, you little shit. Get down here, now, or I'm putting all your origami through the paper shredder."

Okay, so I wasn't exactly being maternal. But 30 seconds later, Edward was standing sheepishly beside me, trying to empty the nuts out of his pockets by dropping them behind his back.

He'd barely ditched the evidence when Grandma and Shelley came trotting across the lawn, with two fat security guards huffing along behind them.

"This would be a great time to leave," Grandma said, breathlessly, as she peeked back at the rapidly approaching uniformed men. No one argued. We scuttled — quickly and silently — to the taxi that was dropping off a family of tourists.

Edward sat quietly on the trip back to the train station — sensing, I suppose, that even one stupid comment would result in certain death.

I leaned back in the seat and tried to get comfortable. Fat chance. I hadn't used a toothbrush or hairbrush since the morning, and hadn't showered since before our disastrous wine tasting the night before. I reeked of curry, and could feel more farts building up. I felt awful — and looked worse. We slowly climbed out of the cab at the Bedford train station and walked over to Grandma's dead car.

"Hi!" Clyde said, as he peeked around the hood, flashing his absolutely gorgeous smile. Yes, it was Clyde Junior.

I spun around to look at Shelley — partly to see her reaction, and partly to hide my oily face from Clyde's view. Shelley was gone. All I could see was her rainbow-covered butt as it disappeared into the train station.

"Clyde! I was expecting your daddy!" Grandma gave Clyde Junior a big hug and a kiss on the cheek.

"He dropped me off on his way to tow a lorry." Clyde grinned sheepishly. "He said if I didn't get your car started, I'd be hitchhiking home."

"A lorry is a truck," Edward piped up.

"Well, that seems a bit harsh!" Grandma said, sounding worried — although she was trying to hide a smile, so I wasn't buying it. "What if this old car had been too dead to save?"

"No worries." Clyde leaned his gorgeous, muscular body back over the engine. "It's just a loose alternator wire."

"You're so handy!" Ugh. It was Shelley. She'd popped into the train station to make herself look natural by slapping on concealer, foundation, blush, eyeliner and, from the looks of things, everything else in her purse. She'd layered on so much mascara, it looked like she'd glued spider legs onto her eyelids.

"So, you'll be driving home with us?" Shelley asked, using that high-pitched voice she thinks makes her sound sexy. "Oh, and I meant to ask...is your girlfriend coming to Auntie Gay's wedding?" Subtle. Really subtle.

"Yes, um...well, yes, I'll be driving with you." I was pleased to see that Clyde was looking at Shelley's face in a confused way. Kind of like he was wondering why she'd glued spider legs onto her eyelids.

"But no girlfriend, no. We broke up." Shelley flashed me her stupid *he's mine* look — her spiders almost quivering with intensity. And I flashed her the snottiest *not a chance* look I could come up with. The battle was on.

Thanks to Clyde's gorgeousness — and his mechanical skills, I suppose — the car finally started. And on the drive home, he wasted no time in getting to the point.

"So, how are you going to keep Grammy out of the care home?" he called out from the front passenger seat. "Time's a ticking, right?"

"Well, we're not telling Mom about this trip — it's been a disaster," I said. "I think we need to tell Auntie Gay to be more tolerant — I mean, really, there's nothing actually *wrong* with having a messy house. We just need to get Grandma some live-in help so the place can stay cleaner and tidier."

Clearly, picking the middle seat in the back of the car had been a mistake. If I glanced left, I could see Edward gawking at me like he'd never met me before. And if I glanced right, I could see Shelley giving me her *Who the hell are you?* look. And if I glanced in Grandma's rear-view mirror, I could see the hurt look on her face. So I stared straight ahead and kept talking.

"I think Auntie Gay figures everyone's life should be as organized and predictable as hers, and it isn't true. She should mind her own business. Getting some live-in help would be a perfect compromise. Then everyone will be happy."

"I didn't realize I needed to make everyone happy in order to stay in my home," Grandma said quietly.

Clyde Junior glanced at Grandma, then reached over and gave her arm a squeeze. She looked at him and smiled sadly.

Edward and Shelley were still drilling holes into my head with their eyes. Probably because — although it pains me to admit it — it was screamingly obvious that I'd just hurt Grandma's feelings. And probably because — although it pains me to admit it — I hadn't exactly been the most tolerant person in the past. And probably because — could this get any worse? — now the summer camp issue had gotten so big it was impossible to ignore. I felt...small.

Thankfully, we pulled up in front of Grandma's house before Shelley could think of anything ignorant to say. I couldn't wait for a shower — a long, steamy shower. Then we could have a bite to eat while we made up a decent story to tell Auntie Gay in the morning. After eight hours of sleep. Or maybe 10.

Grandma threw open the front door and froze. There, on the couch, sat Mom and Auntie Gay. And Auntie Gay's...lips. They were huge. Swollen up like she was a cartoon character. Like she'd been stung by a mob of angry bees. Like...

"Good grief, what happened to your lips?" Edward asked.

"Never mind my lipth," Auntie Gay said — or, at least, tried to say. "What do you have to thay for yourthelf? You're driving me inthane, you know." Auntie Gay glared at Grandma.

This would, of course, have been a great time for a tactful response — something that would diffuse the tension and help everyone relax. Unfortunately, tact was not something Grandma had a lot of.

"You've been *inthane* for years," Grandma said, frowning. "Nobody needs to drive you there. And what happened to your damned lips?"

Chapter 11

Who's Creeping Charlie, Anyway?

"I went to the doctorth today and had my lipth treated for the wedding," Auntie Gay said, as she tried — without much success — to tilt her chin and suck in her lips so they wouldn't look quite so fat.

"She had them filled with collagen," Mom said, as she tried — without much success — to stop her eyes from rolling. "It's a common enough procedure, but not the sort of thing to have done the day before a wedding — it's going to take hours of cold packs to reduce the swelling."

Sadly, Auntie Gay was going to have to find her own cold packs, because Mom never even tossed her a sympathetic glance before turning on us.

"Where on earth did you go?" she asked, just a few decibels short of a full-blown yell (and she can yell, let me tell you). "Auntie Gay had to pick me up at the airport because you'd taken off! What were you thinking? And what were you doing waltzing around London when it was already so crammed with people? And blah! Blah, blah, *blah*, blah, blah..."

I really don't know what she said after that. I kind of tuned it out.

I was tired. Really, really tired. The sort of tired where just sitting upright seems like a lot of work. I guess jet lag, Grandma's homemade wine, the seven minute and 13 second trip through London, the broken-down car, curry poisoning...I guess it all just finally hit me.

So while Grandma, Auntie Gay and Mom yelled at each other, I leaned my head against the back of the couch and counted cats as they took turns poking their fuzzy little heads through the hole in the ceiling.

I'd counted 25 or 26 heads — there'd been a lot of repeats, and Dopey was clearly the most curious of the lot — when I started to actually feel pleased with myself. Here I was sitting in an incredible, 450-year-old house in Old Warden, England. I was half a world away from home and doing just fine.

I felt grown up. I felt empowered. I began to think that I could even bring myself to stand up and do something useful, like get a cold pack out of the freezer for Auntie Gay's monstrous lips. Then I'd make an intelligent comment that would catch everyone's attention. Maybe I'd even say something funny and clever to break the ice so we could have a calm discussion instead of the screaming match about old folks' homes that was going on right now.

I was ready to take action. All I had to do was get my face out of the litter box.

My face. What was my face doing in a litter box? And why was I lying on my side on the couch? Last time I'd checked, I'd been upright. I thrashed my arms wildly, but they wouldn't move. And now that I was waking up, the gassy cat poop smell was getting stronger.

I thrashed some more. Why wouldn't my arms move? My

heart pounded. Had I been in a terrible accident? Was I paralyzed? Suffering from amnesia? I thrashed again. No luck. My arms were completely useless.

"Monica, you idiot, your arms are pinned underneath you," Shelley said. "And get your face out of the cat's butt — that's disgusting."

Sadly, Shelley — possibly the most annoying sister to ever walk the face of the earth — was right. At some point during my cat-counting spree I'd fallen asleep and toppled over onto my side. My arms were pinned underneath me and both of them were now completely numb — which explained why the thrashing hadn't done a bit of good. To make matters worse, one of Grandma's cats had decided to keep his bum warm while he napped by sticking it right up against my nose — hence, the litter box smell.

I flopped around on the couch, trying to push myself upright using my numb arms. Trying to do it super-casually, too, so I wouldn't catch anyone's attention. You don't want people staring at you when you've got your face in a cat's butt and two useless arms.

It took me a minute, but I finally realized the room had grown silent.

"Fine," Grandma said, sighing. "I'll look at the place, but I'm not promising anything. I love my home. Well, *your* home."

Huh?

Grandma was scowling at Auntie Gay.

"I don't understand," I said, staring at Grandma. "This is *your* home. This has always been your home."

An odd silence settled on the room. I tried to keep my arms still as the pins and needles feeling got stronger and more painful.

"It was. Well, it is," said Grandma. "But I signed it over to

Auntie Gay a few years ago, so the government couldn't take it away if they put *me* away."

"Oh, thtop that," Auntie Gay said. "Don't be tho dramatic."

"I don't understand..." I didn't understand. I really didn't. Whose house *was* this?

"Oh, Monica," Mom said, sounding as impatient as she looked. "The government will seize all of Grandma's assets when she goes into a home — all of her money and everything she owns is used to pay for her care. By putting this house in Auntie Gay's name, they were trying to make sure it would stay in the family."

"But who will use it?" I asked. "If Grandma's not in it, who will live here?"

"Well, I will, of courth," Auntie Gay said. "My houth ith too thmall."

"What about Grandma's pets? What about Fred and the cats?"

Mom squirmed. "They'll have to go to the Humane Society," she said. "Auntie Gay's...not really an animal lover."

Auntie Gay scowled. Grandma just looked sad.

My heart was pounding. My armpits were sweating like mad.

I stared at Auntie Gay. "So if Grandma goes into a senior's home, *you* get her house, Fred and the cats all get destroyed and Mom doesn't get any inheritance? This place must be worth half a million!"

Mom squirmed in her seat. "Oh, sweetie, I don't care about the money. And this isn't about what I want, anyway. It's about what Grandma needs — and if this is what she needs, then this is what we do."

I looked down at my hands. It wasn't about what Mom

wanted. It was about what Grandma needed. True. Completely and totally true. It wasn't about what *I* wanted, either. It was about what Grandma needed...

Mom — who didn't have a whole lot of money, to be quite frank — was willing to give up a half million dollar inheritance in order to do the right thing for Grandma. And what was I doing? Trying to win myself a trip to camp — even if it meant doing the wrong thing for Grandma. If I could have disappeared into the couch, I would have.

"You know," I said. "I don't think it's anyone's business how Grandma chooses to live. She doesn't...she doesn't need to live like the rest of us to be okay on her own."

I had to avoid eye contact with Mom, who was a prissy perfectionist, just like me. And Auntie Gay, who looked creepy with her fat lips and intense scowl. *And* Shelley and Edward — who were, no doubt, about to accuse me of being nothing more than a selfish, greedy granddaughter. So I pretty much had to stare at the cat that was now sprawled across my lap.

"It's true, I've always preferred things organized and neat, but Grandma doesn't need to go into a home just because she isn't like that." I scratched the cat behind his ears, making him purr. "If Grandma really wants to stay here, and if she's able to take care of herself, you have no right to say she has to move."

My heart was pounding so hard, I'm pretty sure you could have seen it right through my shirt.

"Monica," Mom rubbed her eyes. "Grandma's 77. The fact that you cleaned out her house before I got here doesn't mean she can take care of herself after we leave."

Auntie Gay nodded. "She'th too old to th-tay here on her own."

"Even complete nutcases get to live on their own if they want to," I mumbled.

"Hey!" Grandma said.

"Sorry, Grandma, I'm just saying...as long as you aren't hurting other people, there's nothing wrong with you living here and keeping the place the way you want it. You can have live-in help if you want, or you can do it all yourself. It really *is* your business."

"You're right, you know," she said, nodding. "And I don't want live-in help. I like my house just the way it is."

Mom turned to Grandma and smiled sadly. "I guess what it comes down to is that I'm worried — really worried. I need to know that you can cope well, without these kids coddling you. But let's make the decision together, okay?"

"She's going to do more than just cope — she's going to amaze you," I blurted out. Proving, once again, that I really need to learn to shut up.

"Aaarrrggghhh..." Apparently, Auntie Gay had hit her limit. "I'm thick of thith," she said. "The rehearthal ith tonight — *don't* be late. I thimply cannot handle any more problemth! No more problemth!"

Auntie Gay stomped dramatically out the door.

"What does she mean about problems?" Edward asked.

"Oh, the bridesmaids dresses aren't done, yet — we won't be getting them 'till tomorrow morning," Grandma said. "And she's gained two stone since spring, so she looks like a sausage in her wedding dress."

"Two stone is 28 pounds," Edward whispered.

Mom glanced at her watch. "Oh *no!* The rehearsal starts at six — we only have an hour to get there!"

It was a frenzied hour, but somehow everyone got showered, Shelley troweled on a fresh layer of makeup, and we made it to the church with three minutes to spare.

"We still have time to give our condolences to the victim," Grandma whispered, as we walked up the church steps.

"Condolences?" Shelley asked. "What victim?"

I rolled my eyes. "The groom," I said. "Who else would Grandma be talking about?"

The victim was just inside the church's massive doors, smiling and shaking hands with everyone as they entered. Hubert. A 68-year-old widow with three grown kids. A kind, gentle old man who clearly deserved so much better than what he was about to get.

"Hello, Hubert," Grandma said, as she shook his hand. "You still have time to change your mind and run away — no one would blame you."

Hubert smiled sweetly. "Her bark is worse than her bite," he whispered. "Don't worry about me, luv."

Truthfully, the wedding rehearsal was a bit of a letdown after the drama that led up to it. It was long, slow and boring ("the warm-up to a traditional English Catholic wedding," Grandma whispered). There was a lot of arm waving and standing and sitting and singing, plus a grumpy old priest who kept correcting all of the non-Catholics who were pretty clueless about what they were supposed to be doing.

I was quite certain that this wedding was going to be a huge yawn.

The one highlight? Auntie Gay had decided to match up the bridesmaids and ushers so we could walk down the aisle in pairs. My usher (proving that there really is a God) was Clyde Junior. Shelley had to walk down the aisle with one of Auntie Gay's neighbors — a boy whose pimples were so big they strained against his skin, shimmering as if the slightest touch would make them explode. It was a truly disgusting display of the evils of puberty, and the sight of Shelley walking down the aisle with Zit Boy was a memory I'll treasure for the rest of my life.

The rehearsal dinner took my breath away — literally. Everyone who was at the rehearsal — plus dozens of their friends and relatives — showed up for a potluck feast in the church garden. Almost all of them were smokers. Heavy smokers, too — the kind that light their next cigarette using the glowing embers of the one still in their mouth. There was no wind, and the smoky haze became so thick I'm surprised my clothes didn't burst into flames.

"Hurry up, for Heaven's sake, we're running low on plates," Auntie Gay hissed as she stomped past me with the potato salad. She'd finally taken the time to put ice packs on her face — she still had fat lips, but she could nag normally, again.

I took fresh plates to the buffet table, and that's where I found Clyde Junior. He was leaning against a fence, staring out over the neighboring fields.

"They picked a great place for a wedding," he said, when he saw me glance in his direction.

"They did, yes." It was true. The church's beautiful back garden opened onto a pasture filled with grazing cows. Large fields bordered by thick green hedges stretched out for miles. "The farmers must love it here."

"Actually, everything you're looking at is owned by one old guy who's gone a bit nutty, from the sounds of it." Clyde smiled. "He has over 100 cattle out there, and he's named every single one of them — says he chooses their names based on their personalities."

Clyde pointed to the one lone bull, which was standing away from the herd, looking in our direction. "That's Creeping Charlie. He's gotta be 28-years-old, now, and not much good for anything, but the old guy won't give him up."

"Creeping Charlie? Why did he call him that?" I asked.

Clyde just shrugged. "There's no telling what some old folk are thinking."

"Hubert, dammit, I told you to empty the ashtrays!" Auntie Gay's shrill voice made us jump.

"Yes," I said, smiling. "There's no telling what some old folk are thinking." Clyde and I grinned at each other, and I savored the warm feeling that comes from sharing a joke with a drop-dead gorgeous guy. It was absolutely, truly and completely The Perfect Moment.

"Monica!" Shelley slithered up beside Clyde, brushing her gigantic boobs against his arm. "Don't hog this guy — he's big enough to share."

Cripes. Even when she was trying to be clever, Shelley still sounded like an idiot.

Edward wandered over, chewing his lip. "My gut feeling..."

"Your gut feeling?" Shelley interrupted. "You're such a science freak, you don't even know what a gut feeling is." It was official: The Perfect Moment had been wrecked.

"My gut feeling," Edward said. "By which I mean my uneducated opinion which shall, henceforth, be blamed upon my digestive tract..."

"You are *such* a freak," Shelley muttered, as she slid even closer to Clyde — leaving, as far as I could tell, just two squished oxygen molecules between them.

"Would you let me finish, please?" Edward frowned. "My gut feeling is that Grandma needs to do something impressive at the wedding. All of Auntie Gay's friends and relations will be there — she'll have to admit that Grandma is perfectly okay if Grandma does something impressive at the wedding."

Then they turned toward me. All three of them — Clyde, Edward and Shelley — stood staring, waiting for *me* to come up with "something impressive."

Sadly, I couldn't think of anything. Not a thing. My only concern at that particular moment was how I was going to get Shelley's boobs away from the guy I was hoping to marry some day.

"Um...how about a speech?" I said, halfheartedly. "She could make a, uh, moving speech at the reception."

"Couldn't she just tell the old battle-ax to move?" Edward asked, wiggling his eyebrows mischievously.

"Or kidnap Hubert to save him from his ghastly fate?" Clyde grinned at me, then casually stepped a few inches away from Shelley's boobs (a simple gesture, but it meant so much).

"Or fill up her lips with even more collagen so she can't talk Hubert's ear off?" I said, laughing.

"Or kick her ungrateful, loathsome young relatives out of her wedding before they attempt to destroy it?"

It was Auntie Gay. Clearly, she'd overheard us. And, clearly, she was not amused.

Chapter 12

Incredibly, It Gets Worse

"We..."

"I..."

"We didn't mean..."

"It wasn't..."

Okay, so we didn't exactly handle the situation with class. But we were making headway — the creases in Auntie Gay's forehead were starting to fade a bit. Then Grandma and Mom sauntered over.

"So, what are you mad about now, you old cow?" Grandma asked, with her usual grace and tact. "The world's still not perfect enough for you, yet?"

Auntie Gay turned on Grandma like she'd found the root cause of all that was evil. "These children are *horrible*!" she yelled. "They're trying to wreck my wedding!"

I thought that was a bit unfair. Clearly, Grandma wasn't thrilled about it, either. "The only thing sure to wreck *your* wedding," Grandma said. "Is the fact that *you're* the bride."

Auntie Gay opened her mouth, but no sound came out. I think she was basically so angry that everything she wanted to yell kind of got jammed up in her throat. Either that, or her puffy, collagen-filled lips just couldn't form the words. (Seriously, they were *huge* — like something you'd see on a cartoon.)

"Aaarrrggghhh..." Auntie Gay said (she'd been saying that a lot, lately), then spun around and stomped toward the nearest clump of guests.

Mom shook her head. "You're driving her nuts, you know."

"It's a short drive," Grandma muttered, as she watched her sister wobble across the lawn on her too-high heels. "She looks ridiculous in those shoes. Her lips look like she's been attacked by killer bees. And she's just too bloody *old* for a big wedding like this. She's acting like a spoiled brat. A spoiled, mummified old brat."

Edward snorted, his brown curls bouncing wildly as he nodded his head.

"Please, Grandma, don't make it any worse," I said, as I jabbed Edward in the ribs. "We need to make you look good so you can stay in your home."

Grandma sighed. "Oh, all right, Monica. But I want you to know you're taking all the fun out of this. What's the point in having a sister if you can't irritate her once in a while?"

I glanced over at Shelley, who was sidling over to Clyde Junior so she could brush her enormous boobs against his arm (again). Truthfully, I didn't see *any* point in having a sister. At least, not one whose bra was four sizes bigger than mine.

Luckily, we got through the rest of the night without any more trouble — basically, by avoiding Auntie Gay and by keeping Grandma busy serving everyone's drinks.

We finally got back to Grandma's house — reeking of cigarette smoke and coughing up chunks of our lungs — at 3 a.m.

"I'll set the alarm for 10:30," Grandma said, as she shuffled off to her room. "That should give us enough time to get back to the church before the old battle-ax comes searching for us."

What it *wouldn't* give us was enough time for a decent night's sleep, but I was too tired to care. It felt like my head had just hit the pillow when I started having a weird dream about someone banging on the wall, yelling something about morning...about hurrying up...about being more responsible...just yelling, basically. And banging. A lot of banging. It wasn't a pleasant dream.

It wasn't a dream, either.

"Oh, for God's sake, woman, it's only 8 o'clock," I heard Grandma yell. "This is a wedding — not a bloody coronation!"

I opened my eyes. But just a quick peek — I wasn't sure I could handle a full blast of sunlight.

Oddly, there was no sun. Only darkness. Big, hairy, smelly darkness. Fred — who had his usual thick line of bubbly drool dangling from his lower lip — was leaning in close, staring intently at my face. And as soon as he saw my eyes flutter, he leaned in even closer, snuffling loudly (looking, no doubt, for the ideal place to wipe the toilet water off his mouth).

I scrambled backward, trying to get away from his slimy face.

Bad move. I'd been sleeping right at the edge of the bed. One scramble and I was no longer *on* the bed — I was airborne. Then, just as quickly, I was flat on my back on the hard wooden floor, sharp pains shooting up my neck.

"The *Queen* has brought your gowns," Grandma yelled up the stairs. "Come see."

Well, she didn't have to call *me* twice. I'd seen the way Auntie Gay dressed. I could imagine the horror that was waiting for us.

Turns out I couldn't.

When I got to the bottom of the stairs — with Shelley, Mom and Edward trailing behind me — I couldn't even make sense of what I was seeing. The couch was covered — absolutely covered — with enormous piles of black and white stripes. Or flowers. Black and white flowers. Stripes of flowers? My head was still throbbing. Was this an optical illusion, or a sign of permanent brain damage?

"What the..." Mom — who's *never* at a loss for words — was at a loss for words.

Grandma smiled, then slowly picked up a fistful of flowers, or stripes, or whatever they were, and held them up. It was a dress. A huge, flowing, floor-length dress with long sleeves, a *very* low-cut neckline and a tiny — alarmingly tiny — waist. It was a dress absolutely covered with shiny black and white cloth flowers. In horizontal rows, no less — big fat rows of black flowers and big fat rows of white flowers circling around a big fat poofy floor length dress with a ridiculously small waist and low-cut neckline.

Somebody had shot and skinned three morbidly obese zebras. I was in hell.

We stood, silent, trying to absorb the shock.

"Let's see how they look on you." Grandma was trying to keep a straight face — and doing a terrible job of it. "Put them on."

So we did. Instead of running away. Instead of suddenly developing a bad case of the flu. Instead of having an appendicitis attack. Instead of doing something — *anything* — that would have gotten us out of this wedding, we put the dresses on. Then we stood in a circle, facing each other. Three enormous, bloated, frilly zebras.

"Cripes, I'm roasting," Shelley said, as she tried to squish her boobs down into the bodice of her dress. "What's this thing made of?"

"Insulation, as far as I can tell," muttered Mom, who already had sweat trickling down her forehead.

If you'd asked me — before seeing that dress — to design an outfit that would look terrible on every single woman, no matter what her shape or size, I would have said it was impossible.

I would have been wrong.

This dress looked awful on Mom — the tiny waist pinched so much in the middle that it made her wide hips swell out like two enormous black and white striped balloons. It looked awful on Shelley — her massive boobs bulged out of the low-cut neckline and bounced around like two overfilled bowls of jelly. And it looked awful on me — the bodice hung loosely in front of my flat chest, making it obvious that my body had decided to not bother growing breasts at all.

"I look *fabulous*!" Edward announced. He was standing on the coffee table, holding out his arms and turning in slow circles, modeling the tuxedo Auntie Gay had left for him. It fit beautifully, and the simple white shirt and black bow tie made him look like a tiny groom. It made me sick to admit it, but the little snot *did* look fabulous.

"She also wants you to wear these." Grandma held up white, pointy-toed, ridiculously high-heeled shoes — shoes designed to cripple, as well as to impress. "Oh, and those," she added, as she pointed to a big box on the couch, while trying to avoid eye contact with us.

I shuffled over to the box. Slowly. The dress was so bulky and hot I felt like I'd been wrapped in heating pads and then covered with plastic.

The box. I wasn't the least bit surprised to see that it contained things we would be expected to wear on our heads — thick plastic circles (like mini hula hoops) covered with fake black and white flowers, plus ridiculously long strands of black and white ribbon dangling down the back.

"Shoot me now," Shelley muttered, as she wobbled across the living room to the nearest mirror. Even Shelley — the Fashion Goddess — couldn't walk properly in heels that high.

I glanced over at Grandma. She was sitting on the couch with two cats curled up in her lap, sipping a cup of tea and watching us with an amused look on her face.

Grandma was smart and funny and healthy and wickedly good at chess. Yet I'd gotten swept up in trying to put her into a home. And why? Because she collected too much and cleaned too little. Big deal. Judging by the freakish outfit I was wearing, Auntie Gay was the one who was losing her marbles and needed to be tossed into a home. It was time to make things right. I could go to science camp another year.

Suddenly, there was a loud knock at the door. I looked up just in time to see Clyde Junior — breathtaking, gorgeous Clyde Junior — walk in. He was carrying one of Grandma's huge, fuzzy cats, and was wearing one of his huge, gorgeous smiles.

"Did you lose one of the seven dwarfs last ni..." It was as if someone had clicked the pause button on the TV remote. Clyde just stood there, staring. Frozen on the spot. Only his eyebrows were still moving. They were quivering — like they desperately wanted to shoot right off his forehead to register their alarm.

"You look, um...you, you look...you...here's your cat!" And with that, the man that I was going to have to walk down the aisle with in less than five hours set the snarly creature on the floor and scuttled out the door backward, staring intently at his own feet as if he'd never seen them before.

"Shall we go to the church now?" Edward asked, trying hard to keep a serious look on his face. Trying so hard, in fact, that he looked constipated. And after a quick round of hair brushing and make-up application, there was really no way to avoid it.

"Lead the way, you little snot," Shelley muttered, as we wobbled out the door.

Without a word, we climbed into Grandma's car. It was a small car, and our dresses were poofy. So poofy, in fact, that Edward's head was the only part of him sticking up above the sea of black and white flowers in the back seat. It was a long, silent drive.

"Oh, Lord, she's at it again," Grandma muttered, as she climbed out of her car at the church. We could already hear Auntie Gay shrieking inside.

"Can I go exploring?" Edward asked.

"Fine, just don't get dirty," Mom muttered as she tried, for the millionth time, to pull the front of her dress up high enough to cover her bra.

We wobbled into the church, and directly into a tornado of stress. Half a dozen people I'd never met were racing around at top speed, doing whatever the screeching bride commanded. And the screeching bride? *She* was standing on a chair in the middle of the lobby, with two women squatting down at her ankles, frantically hemming her wedding dress.

The dress. Incredibly, Auntie Gay had managed to top everything I'd seen her wear so far. Her wedding dress had clearly been made using the same pattern as ours. It was just as long, just as poofy, and had just as low a neckline. But *her* fake, shiny flowers were all white. Shockingly, blindingly white. She looked like an albino zebra — an albino zebra wearing blood-red lipstick and screaming at everyone who made eye contact, plus a lot of the people who were trying hard not to.

"You're late," she snapped, as she climbed down off the chair. "Go see Edith — she's doing your hair."

"Edith? Who's Edith?" Shelley whispered, as we scuttled down the hall. "And what's she going to *do* to our hair?"

"You probably don't want to know," Grandma said, as she stomped off with an armload of candles.

Fifteen minutes later, we knew. Edith — who was so old that her hands shook uncontrollably — had been instructed by the screeching bride to give us "up-do's."

So she soaked our hair with industrial-strength hairspray — the kind that hardens into a certified bike helmet if you put it on thickly enough. Then she brushed it straight up, rolled the sticky strands into tight little curls, and jammed the flowery, ribbony head things back on top of the whole mess. We'd been shellacked.

"This is the worst day of my life," Shelley muttered, as she picked at the stray hairs that were stuck to her cheeks. "I'm not going through with this."

I nodded. I tried to, anyway — there was so much hairspray on my neck, I could feel the skin pull every time I moved my head.

"I'm with Shelley. This stinks," I said, proving that people really do pull together in the face of disaster.

Suddenly, Mom — looking like an enraged zebra — turned on us. "I paid for four plane tickets, took time off work, flew all the way over here and got into this hideous outfit. You're going through with this damned wedding, is that clear?"

"Mom…" It was Edward. He'd run into the room at top speed, and was now tugging frantically on Mom's arm.

"And you'll act like you're happy about it," she said, ignoring tux boy.

"Mom…" More tugging.

"And you can stop whining about these stupid outfits. If I have to put up with this, you bloody well will, too." Mom tried to scowl, but — thanks to Edith's hand tremors — her forehead was coated with as much hairspray as the back of my neck.

"Mom..." The tugging was starting to annoy *me*, and it wasn't even my arm.

Whooomp...

The explosion made the windows rattle. Then the lights went out and we were plunged into a dusky, colorful sort of gloom that you only get when sunlight streams through old stained glass windows.

"Edward," Mom said, using her best I'm-trying-to-be-calm voice. "What did you do?"

"I...I think I may have set the church on fire," he replied.

Chapter 13

So That's Why They Call Him
Creeping Charlie

"I wanted to try lighting the furnace — it's one of those antique ones where you can actually see the flame in the fire box," Edward explained, as Auntie Gay's helpers scrambled out the front door of the church. "I couldn't get it lit, so I hit the reset button. That's when I realized the chimney was already full of oil — which is generally the beginning of a really big explosion."

Generally, yes...but it didn't take long to figure out that Edward hadn't *really* set the church on fire. The explosion had been impressive, but all it had done was blow the electrical panel off the wall. It would be dark until an electrician replaced the panel, but at least no one was hurt. All in all, it really wasn't that big a deal.

"*This* is the *worst* day of my life," Auntie Gay screamed, making both Mom and Grandma roll their eyes. She'd changed into the bright orange robe and slippers that she'd been wearing the night she caught us in her tree — and her hair was full of the same huge green rollers, too. She looked as frightful now as she had back then.

"Don't get yourself into a lather," Grandma said. "You made me buy all those stupid candles — we'll just make this a candlelit wedding."

"And we can pee in the bushes like we're camping!" Edward added.

For, quite possibly, the millionth time in his short life, all eyes turned toward Edward.

"Well...I mean...you see, we're in the middle of the country, so the church must get its water from a well," Edward said, squirming a bit as the enormity of what he was saying finally sunk in. "The well pump needs electricity, so the toilets and sinks aren't going to work until the electrical panel is fixed."

"This *is* the worst day of my life," Auntie Gay screamed dramatically. Again. "And *you* are the nastiest little..."

I really don't want to repeat everything she said. To summarize: the wedding was going to be a dismal failure, it was *all our fault*, and we were going to go to hell for it. I'm paraphrasing, but that was the gist of it.

True, it was all a bit harsh, but the fact that she had lipstick smeared on her teeth, grass stains on her slippers, and was standing right beside an enormous pile of cow poop kind of took the sting out of her insults.

Still screaming, Auntie Gay led the reluctant guests back into the church, while Mom and Grandma scuttled off to search for matches. Soon, Shelley and I were the only ones left outside.

I stared out across the calm, quiet fields of grazing cows. Creeping Charlie was standing with his back to us, about 60 yards away, gazing off into the distance and calmly chewing his cud. It was so peaceful, I felt my shoulders finally relax.

"I have to pee," Shelley said — once again, wrecking the mood.

"You didn't a few minutes ago," I muttered.

"Well, I have to go now."

"It's all in your head, you know. You only feel like you have to go because you know the toilets won't flush. Go pee in a bush."

"Come with me. I don't want to go out there alone." Shelley hiked up her dress and headed toward the nearest clump of trees.

"What are you afraid of? Cows are herbivores — they don't eat zebras." I thought that was pretty clever, actually, but Shelley just glared at me and kept walking. I looked out across the muddy field. Creeping Charlie was standing about 50 yards away, lazily swatting flies with his tail.

I sighed and lifted up the hem of my dress. It was quite a hike to the trees — not in terms of distance, but in terms of effort. Our heels kept getting stuck in the dirt, and the poofy dresses were surprisingly hard to hold up — yet we couldn't let them drag, of course, or they'd end up streaked with mud and cow poop.

When we finally reached the long row of trees, I leaned against the first one while Shelley checked out all the others — looking for the perfect one to pee behind, I guess.

"Just *go*," I said, as I glanced across the field. Creeping Charlie was standing about 15 yards away, still absent-mindedly chewing, still gazing out over his harem of cows.

"Gimme a break, Monica. Cripes."

"What's your problem?" I asked.

"I need a break from you. From your criticizing and complaining. I just need a break."

I stood staring at Shelley as she tried to hike her dress up high enough to squat and pee. *She* needed a break from *me*?

Shelley glared at me. "You're not exactly a dream to live with, you know. You're very judgmental. You could ease up on us a bit. A *lot*, actually."

Huh. *She* needed a break from *me*...

Suddenly, I felt a twinge. "Oh, cripes, now *I* have to go." I stepped behind a tree and lifted my dress.

"It's all in your head, you know," Shelley said, in her snottiest voice. "You only feel like you have to go because you know the toilets won't flush."

I glared at her, trying to ignore how stupid we looked — two girls with stiff, hairspray-soaked ringlets, enormous dresses hiked up to our waists and underwear bunched up around our ankles, squatting to avoid peeing on our high-heeled shoes.

I'd just pulled my underwear back up when I felt the ground shake. Then something slammed into me. Hard. I don't remember my feet leaving the ground, but I do remember landing — and then skidding — face down, through a puddle of mud. Stabbing pains shot across my side.

"Monica, look out!" Shelley screamed — a little late, I thought.

I lifted my head just in time to see Creeping Charlie leaning over me. Before I could get to my feet, he licked the side of my face with his enormous, sandpapery tongue, and then started chomping loudly on the fake flowers in my hair.

I'd have been happy to give him the whole flowery head thing, but Edith had tacked it down using at least 20 bobby pins — if Creeping Charlie pulled it out, he'd take most of my hair with it.

"Shelley, do something!" I tried scrambling backward through the mud. No luck. Creeping Charlie had sucked most of my ringlets into his mouth along with the flowers.

Suddenly, he snorted loudly and let go. As I jumped to my

feet, I saw a flash of dark hair. Clyde Junior! He'd grabbed Creeping Charlie's nose ring and was twisting his head away from me. And with a strong kick, Clyde persuaded the beast to lumber away.

"Oh, Monica," Shelley said. "You look like hell."

It wasn't tactful, but it was true. My knees, elbows and ribs were badly bruised. My dress was splattered with mud, and — from what I could see of the frayed, dangling ribbons — my flowery head thing was ruined, as well. I gently patted my hair and groaned. Creeping Charlie had mangled Edith's handiwork — long strands of sticky hair fanned out, peacock-style. Clyde stared — his expression bouncing between amusement and concern — as I groped for something to say.

"Um...thank you." I tried not to flinch as I touched my ribs. "He really nailed me."

"I guess that's why they call him Creeping Charlie. He likes to sneak up on people." Clyde stifled a smile as he glanced over at the bull.

Creeping Charlie stared at us calmly from across the field as he licked fake flower petals off his lips.

"You're going to have quite a story to tell the other wedding guests," Clyde said.

The wedding! A quick glance at my watch told me I was probably doomed — it was already 12:30 and the wedding was supposed to start at 1 o'clock. It was going to take a miracle to get me cleaned up in time.

Once again, Shelley and I hiked up our dresses and headed across the field. But this time we waddled along as fast as our spiky heels would carry us, mud splattering up dangerously close to our hemlines.

"She's going to kill you, you know," Shelley said, as she gasped for air. "This *will* be the last straw."

"Everything's the last straw with her," I muttered, as we staggered into the church. "Clyde, do you know where the washrooms are?"

Shelley stomped her feet on the doormat, splattering clumps of dried mud across the entryway. I didn't even bother trying — my shoes were coated with wet, sticky sludge from the puddle I'd skidded through.

"Follow me." Clyde pounded down the basement stairs into the gloom — then, just as quickly, pounded back up. "Hang on..."

Barely one minute later, he was back — this time, carrying a flashlight. "*Now*, follow me!"

Down the stairs we staggered, following the flashlight's yellow glow. At the bathroom door, Clyde stopped and handed me the light. "Good luck," he said.

"She's going to need more than luck," Shelley muttered.

I raced into the bathroom and turned on the tap. Of course, I kind of knew it wouldn't work — had almost known for absolute certain that it wouldn't work. But it wasn't until I *saw* that it wouldn't work — saw the tap sputter and then fall silent — that I knew my trek to hell was complete.

"Well, that's it, then." Shelley leaned against the wall. "You're screwed."

I stood there staring at the useless tap, my heart heavy and stomach tight. This was my last chance to do anything to help Grandma. This was my last chance to fix the mess that I'd...well...not *started*, but that I'd gotten involved in and made worse. This was my last chance to do something to actually help Grandma, without being selfish and judgmental. I *had* to look normal — or, at least, as normal as possible under the circumstances — so I could get out there and do something.

Suddenly, I had an idea. A disgusting, hideous, nauseating idea. An idea that just might work.

I handed Shelley the flashlight. "Point it at the toilet," I said, as I took a deep breath — possibly my last — and headed over to the old, cracked, rust-stained relic.

"*What* are you doing?" Shelley asked, as she followed me with the light.

I didn't answer — couldn't, actually, because I was holding my breath. I lifted the lid off the back tank and peered in. Water. Toilet water. I hate toilet water.

"I'm going to wash my face, my neck and my hands, scrub the mud off these shoes and then fix my hair."

I wasn't really saying it out loud to convince Shelley — I was saying it out loud to convince *me*. For as long as I could remember, I'd always done things the *right* way — the clean, organized, tidy way. Well, now it was time to do the right *thing* — even if it meant a pretty major dose of yuck. And this was — I have to say it — a pretty major dose of yuck.

"That's disgusting. Don't you dare."

"It isn't disgusting," I said — once again, trying to convince myself more than her. "This water is clean — it hasn't been through the toilet bowl, yet."

"It's *in* the toilet, you idiot," she snapped. "It's toilet water."

I sighed. "Then today, I wash my face in the toilet."

I grabbed the dried-up, cracked bar of soap that was on the counter and plunged it into the tank (the water was shockingly cold). Then, with my eyes and lips shut so tightly that even oxygen molecules couldn't squeeze through, I splashed water on my face and neck and started to scrub.

"Oh, Monica! That's disgusting!" Shelley screamed, jumping up and down, leaving me in darkness as the pale beam of light bounced off the walls.

"You're being stupid," I snapped. "It's the same water that comes out of the tap." Which was true, but I still had to fight the urge to throw up as I washed the mud off my lips.

"Follow me with the light." I headed toward the mirror. "I have to fix my hair."

Truthfully, there wasn't much I could do with it. The curls had been sucked straight by Creeping Charlie, and he'd chewed at least half the fake flowers and ribbons off the hula-hoop thing.

But my hair was now soaked in bull spit, which turned out to be almost as strong as hair gel. I quickly mushed my hair upwards and twirled it into a tight little bun, then used Edith's bobby pins to hold it in place and stuck what was left of the headdress back on top.

When we stepped out of the bathroom, Clyde Junior was waiting. He took the flashlight and shone it on me, calmly looking me up and down.

"Doesn't she look ridiculous?" Shelley asked, as she leaned close to Clyde — proving, once again, that I would have been infinitely happier as an only child.

"Well, no one's perfect," he finally said. "But Monica's still the prettiest girl in town — and she has way more class than anyone else at this silly wedding." Proving, once again, that this was the man I was destined to marry.

Shelley stomped dramatically up the stairs, and Clyde and I followed slowly behind her. My stomach hopped along at its own speed, a sickening bundle of butterflies and knots and half-digested food.

Even with the candles lit, the church was dingy and dark. Maybe — just maybe — no one would realize my mascara was smeared, my shoes were wrecked, my dress was splattered with mud and my hair was being held in place with bull spit. I could always hope.

The organist started playing the wedding march and we quickly paired up (me with Clyde, Shelley with Zit Boy and Mom with Edward). Not surprisingly, there was a fair amount of shoulder bumping and toe stepping, since Mom, Edward and Zit Boy were staring intently at me, instead of at where they were supposed to be going.

"I got attacked by a bull," I whispered, hoping to shut down their multitude of questions before we walked down the aisle.

Thanks to the church's gloomy darkness, I made it to the altar without getting too many second glances from the guests. In fact, at the sight of our enormous zebra dresses, most eyes rocketed to the back of the church, no doubt hoping to see what frightful design the bride had chosen for *her* outfit.

Auntie Gay stepped through the door in her massive, albino zebra dress. She calmly glanced around the church, smiling sweetly at her guests as she walked slowly down the aisle on the arm of her groom.

But when she caught sight of me, her expression changed. Her eyes raced from my hair down to my feet and back up again, then locked onto my eyes, drilling into me like tiny brown torpedoes.

And the instant she reached the altar, it started. "What the hell happened to you?" she hissed. "Haven't you done enough to ruin my special day?" She was still smiling — people were watching, you see — but her words spewed out like acid.

"I was attacked by a bull behind the church," I whispered.

"A bull...*bullshit!*" she whispered, still smiling. "You did this on purpose. You children are evil little trolls."

She was absolutely fuming. She was so ticked off, in fact, that even the priest looked nervous. Instead of stopping constantly to make sure we were all standing and sitting and waving and whatever else at the right times, he raced through his whole spiel at an alarming pace.

The wedding took only half as long as the rehearsal, and soon we were watching poor Hubert kiss his angry bride — a sight that will give me nightmares for years.

Auntie Gay had arranged for photos to be taken outside, and within minutes of spilling out into the sunlight, all eyes were focused on me — and all eyebrows were quivering with questions.

"Okay, spill the beans," one guest called out. "What mud puddle were *you* playing in?"

"Oh, Monica was attacked by a bull," Auntie Gay said, in her sweetest voice. "Wasn't she brave to still join us after such a scary experience?"

I glanced at Grandma, baffled.

Grandma saw my confused expression, and leaned in close. "Appearances are everything to the old cow," she whispered. "She *has* to look good in front of her friends."

I felt goose bumps on the back of my neck. This was my chance — I had to take it.

"Um, I would like to make an announcement," I said, in the loudest voice I could muster. My heart was fluttering, almost skipping beats.

"Monica?" Auntie Gay's torpedo eyes were drilling holes right into my brain. "Are you sure you're up to talking right now?"

"Yes. I want to make an announcement." I took a deep, shaky breath.

"I would like to thank Auntie Gay for helping our Grandma out of her terrible...predicament." My mind raced as I tried to figure out what to say next. "I'd like to thank her for encouraging Grandma to stay in her own beautiful house, instead of moving into a senior's home."

Auntie Gay stood frozen on the spot. Only her eyes moved, flitting rapidly between me and her crowd of guests. If she could have killed me right there, I'm sure she would have done it. I took another deep breath.

"She helped Grandma sort through her things and get organized. She's even offered to clean Grandma's house top to bottom before leaving for her honeymoon. Thanks to her, Grandma's going to do just fine living on her own."

Auntie Gay's friends and family made appreciative oohing and aahing noises and applauded loudly. Mom, Shelley and Grandma stood staring at me, their expressions bouncing between surprise, confusion and amazement.

Auntie Gay smiled thinly — as thinly as a person can smile with puffy, collagen-packed lips — and nodded at the crowd.

"I'm delighted to help my dear sister," she said. Then she turned to me. "And I'll be delighted to wring your scrawny little neck when I get you alone," she whispered — still smiling, of course.

EPILOGUE

Well, Auntie Gay never got a chance to wring my scrawny little neck. It took her three solid days to scrub out that old house — it was small, but packed with a mansion's-worth of dust and cobwebs.

She couldn't get *out* of the job, either, because her friends kept dropping in to see how things were going. It was the first time I'd seen her in pants — and, hopefully, the last (some people should never wear leggings).

When the cleaning was done, Hubert whisked Auntie Gay off for a weeklong honeymoon in Paris (where, rumor has it, she terrorized the hotel staff and complained nonstop about the restaurant service).

We spent a few more days visiting Grandma before flying home. And as if curry dinners weren't enough culinary drama for one summer, Grandma conned us into trying blood pudding (which tastes as bad as it sounds) and toad in a hole (which tastes a lot better than it sounds).

Clyde Junior and I promised to stay in touch, and Facebook a fair bit. I may not end up marrying him, but he's definitely my back-up plan if I haven't found a guy who's as perfect as him by my 20th birthday.

Oh, and I ended up going to science camp, even though I failed completely (and on purpose) at getting Grandma into a senior's home. "You got that mess settled, and Auntie Gay's stopped screaming at us," Mom said. "That's good enough for me."

Other than that, everything's pretty much back to normal. Just yesterday, old Mrs. Frieson was pounding on our door, yelling that Edward was making faces at her from the bathroom.

I went upstairs to check it out and, sure enough, there he was — wearing his polka dot bandana and standing on the toilet with his scrawny little chest hanging out the window. He was naked, of course.

A message from the author:

If you enjoyed *The Day I Washed My Face in the Toilet*, I'd be incredibly grateful if you posted a quick review on Amazon. Even a review of only a few sentences is a great help! And if you have any questions, you can reach me at **brenda@brendakearns.com**. Thank you!

Made in the USA
Middletown, DE
10 December 2015